The Sewing & Afternoon Tea

De-ann Black

Toffee Apple Publishing

Other books in the Sewing, Knitting & Baking book series are:

Book 1 - The Tea Shop.
Book 2 - The Sewing Bee & Afternoon Tea.
Book 3 - The Christmas Knitting Bee.
Book 4 – Champagne Chic Lemonade Money.
Book 5 – The Vintage Sewing & Knitting Bee.

Text copyright © 2018 by De-ann Black
Cover Design & Illustration © 2018 by De-ann Black

All rights reserved.
No part of this book may be used or reproduced in any manner whatsoever without the written consent of the publisher.

This is a work of fiction. Names, characters, places, and incidents are either products of the author's imagination or are used fictitiously. Any resemblance to actual persons, living or dead, businesses, companies, events, or locales is entirely coincidental.

First published 2014

Published by Toffee Apple Publishing 2018

The Sewing Bee & Afternoon Tea

ISBN: 9781976990168

Toffee Apple Publishing

Also by De-ann Black (Romance, Action/Thrillers & Children's books). See her Amazon Author page or website for further details about her books, screenplays, illustrations, art and fabric designs.
www.De-annBlack.com

Romance:
The Sewing Shop
Heather Park
The Tea Shop by the Sea
The Bookshop by the Seaside
The Sewing Bee
The Quilting Bee
Snow Bells Wedding
Snow Bells Christmas
Summer Sewing Bee
The Chocolatier's Cottage
Christmas Cake Chateau
The Beemaster's Cottage
The Sewing Bee By The Sea
The Flower Hunter's Cottage
The Christmas Knitting Bee
The Sewing Bee & Afternoon Tea
The Vintage Sewing & Knitting Bee
Shed In The City
The Bakery By The Seaside
Champagne Chic Lemonade Money
The Christmas Chocolatier
The Christmas Tea Shop & Bakery
The Vintage Tea Dress Shop In Summer
Oops! I'm The Paparazzi
The Bitch-Proof Suit

Action/Thrillers:
Love Him Forever.
Someone Worse.
Electric Shadows.
The Strife Of Riley.
Shadows Of Murder.

Children's books:
Faeriefied.
Secondhand Spooks.
Poison-Wynd.
Wormhole Wynd.
Science Fashion.
School For Aliens.

Colouring books:
Summer Garden. Spring Garden. Autumn Garden. Sea Dream.
Festive Christmas. Christmas Garden. Flower Bee. Wild Garden.
Faerie Garden Spring. Flower Hunter. Stargazer Space. Bee Garden.

Embroidery books:
Floral Nature Embroidery Designs
Scottish Garden Embroidery Designs

Contents

1 - A Cottage in the City	1
2 - A Passion For Sewing	10
3 - Bumblebees & Afternoon Tea	20
4 - Chocolate Daisies	31
5 - Fashion, Fabric & Flirting	41
6 - Cornwall, London & Paris	49
7 - Fairy Cakes & Tea Quilts	58
8 - Sewing Bee Dresses	68
9 - Seaside Sewing	77
10 - The Cocktail Dress Fabrics	84
11 - Pincushions & Quilts	92
12 - Sewing & Baking Cakes	102
13 - Tea Dresses & Busy Bees	108
14 - Romantic Vintage	117
About De-ann Black	126

Chapter One

A Cottage In The City

I cycled through the centre of Glasgow at 6:30 p.m. on a Monday night. The April showers had quit around the same time I'd finished work for the day at teatime. The streets were still wet and glistened in the mellow glow of the evening.

A mild breeze hinted that the end of April was due to give way to a lovely warm May. My ponytail blew behind me like pale blonde ribbons and I caught a glimpse of myself in the shop windows. Dressed in leggings, training shoes and a chunky jumper, I looked younger than my thirty years. The sense of adventure showed on my face, giving colour to my pale complexion.

This was only the second outing on my vintage bike. I'd bought it in the January sales and taken it for a spin around the streets on a frosty New Year night. My boyfriend, Gavyn, an accountant, had scolded me when I skidded to a halt outside the entrance to his flat. Our flat, but his flat.

'Don't be silly, Morag. Put the bike away. You can't cycle round the streets at this time of the year. You're an accident waiting to happen. Wait until the spring when the weather's milder.'

And so I'd waited.

My lovely vintage bike had sat in the hallway of the flat since then. Sometimes I glanced at it as I went in and out of the flat, but as the weeks went by I'd become accustomed to it sitting there and it had become part of the decor. Most days I never even gave it a second glance. I'd been so busy with work. I worked for myself as a freelance artist. I did okay.

However, for the past two years, since around the time I'd first started dating Gavyn, I'd been creating patterns for dressmaking and quilting. I'd also been sending my pattern designs to fabric and pattern manufacturers hoping to secure a contract to design patterns for them. And finally...I'd done it.

Earlier in the day I'd received an offer from a company who made patterns for dressmaking and soft furnishings. They wanted me to create two collections of designs for them. New, exclusive designs. I'd agreed, and signed the contract. An upfront payment for half the money, which was the most I'd ever earned at one time, was winging its way into my bank account.

I was so excited and couldn't wait to tell Gavyn. I'd planned to make his favourite dinner and break the great news that evening. But he was working late, again. He'd phoned to tell me that he had a dinner meeting with clients and that I shouldn't work too hard. I should put my feet up and relax and watch a film. Or have an early night.

I worked most evenings, at least part of the evening, painting and sketching new designs while Gavyn entertained himself online. He was passionate about social media and most nights when he was home he was never really there. Not with me anyway. With them. Chatting, blogging, and all that. I didn't know any of them. And so I worked while he was busy with them.

Anyway, when he'd phoned I decided I'd wait to tell him the news in person so that he could get the full benefit of me jumping up and down with glee.

Bursting with excitement, I hadn't been able to sit still, and that's when the women's magazine article sprang to mind. I'd snipped the article out and stuck it on the side of the kitchen cabinet. It said something along the lines of: this year do something every week just for you. Something you'd love to do, within your budget, capabilities, and without doing anything dangerous or going to places leading to deep, dark danger.

I'm probably exaggerating, or perhaps not. But the gist of it sprang to mind when I walked through to the hall and saw the bike. What would I really like to do? And the answer was — cycle round the streets in the centre of Glasgow.

It was barely 6:30 p.m. and the evenings were becoming lighter as the spring edged on to the beginning of summertime. I planned to cycle through the centre of Glasgow, avoiding all the really busy streets, and keeping away from any that would lead to deep, dark danger. In other words, I kept to the main areas and zipped past the big shop windows, admiring the displays. I felt like I was a young girl again, that my mum had cooked my dinner, I'd no homework and no school the next day, and I'd gone out to play on my bike. The sense of freedom was great. No responsibilities. Of course, those carefree days were long gone. Now there was only me left in my world. Gavyn and me.

We'd been dating for two years and for the past year I'd been living with him at his stylish flat in the city. He'd suggested I move in with him, that it was uneconomical to pay for my flat when I could live with him. The accountant in him never quit. He was quite well–off and I earned okay money, though sometimes my earnings were dismal, so sharing his flat made sense. Why pay for the rent on my little flat when I could move in and pay half of the rent on his? It wasn't much of a money saver for me, but it was certainly a nice feeling taking a step closer to being a couple.

I'd almost done a full circuit of the city centre and started heading back to the flat when I realised I'd only been out for about twenty minutes. I decided to double–back and take a detour up one of the main streets, gazing in the shop windows, seeing them lit up in the early evening as I peddled past. Yes, this was the life. I could see myself getting acquainted with these night cycling escapades especially as the summer was almost here.

I could get fitter, unwind and feel like I was doing something exhilarating. I was reasonably fit and had a slim build mainly from working long hours and forgetting to stop for lunch and dinner when I was on a roll making my designs.

I picked up my pace and whizzed along another street and at the far end of it I saw a yellow car. There weren't many yellow cars in the city. Gavyn's car was yellow. I thought he must have parked outside one of the restaurants where he was having the dinner meeting with clients.

I decided to cycle past and give him a cheery wave if I could see him. Yes, there he was in his nice business suit, brown hair combed neatly back. He was seated at a table one place back from the window. The window table had a reserved sign. I couldn't see any other accountants from his firm. Only him — and her.

I stopped and got off my bike. I blinked as I gazed at them together. They didn't see me. They saw only each other.

She was very attractive, well–dressed, a sophisticated brunette, around the same age as me, perhaps younger. That was my first thought. My second and third thoughts overlapped, clashing together — was this a business meeting and why did I feel like my world was falling away from me?

The answers appeared right in front of me. He smiled at her and she laughed as they sat opposite each other at the table for two having dinner, an intimate, candlelit dinner. Then he leaned across and kissed her. Sweet and passionate.

I let go of the handlebars and the bike fell to the ground, undamaged, unlike me. I'd shattered into a thousand pieces.

Without realising, I stepped forward, pressed my hands against the window and screamed at him, at her, at the world. At the world that had just crumbled around me.

He came running out of the restaurant with his immaculate silk tie flapping in the rush to reach me, console me and shut me up. Mainly the latter as I screeched at him, accusing him of being a two–timing, lying, cheating bastard. I couldn't remember the last time I'd unleashed such raw anger. Perhaps never.

He had the nerve to argue with me. Oh, so it was my fault? We'd drifted and I hadn't done anything to stop the rot so he'd found solace in her manicured clutches. We started to fight and all the resentments he'd harboured came pouring out, hot and vicious. Such bitter accusations from the man I'd been sharing my life with, not knowing how deep his resentment was entrenched.

Then the fight quickly moved up a notch from verbal to 'duck that one you bastard.' He did, but I got him on the second one. An upper–cut to his defiant jaw that sent him reeling backwards. He got up from the ground, rubbed his jaw and glared at me.

And all the while she sat there in the restaurant, smiling to herself, waiting for our relationship to be over which was obviously what she'd wanted for a while. If I'd been her I'd have run out to defend him, to fight me, but no, he'd chosen sexy sophistication above home–loving and loyal. Good luck with that choice.

I picked up my bike and got on it. 'Don't come home until Thursday night,' I shouted at him and cycled out of his life forever.

I didn't know what I was going to do. I only knew that I had to find somewhere else to live. I wept for over an hour and then made myself a strong cup of tea and tried to sort things out.

I went online and searched through properties to rent in the city. I couldn't concentrate so I made another cup of tea, bursting into tears when I saw the remnants of the life I'd shared with Gavyn around me; the food that I'd bought earlier to make his dinner hoping to delight him with my contract news.

I managed to make a cup of tea and as I poured in the milk I saw the article stuck to the side of the kitchen cabinet. I sipped my tea and thought to myself — where would I like to live? Where would I *really* like to live?

I went back online and trawled through *houses with a garden* for rent and found several in the Glasgow area, and one, just one, in the centre of the city.

The photographs of the cottage–style house looked lovely. A cottage in the city? I checked the description. Yes, definitely smack in the city centre, like a piece of the past left standing amid the metropolis. A defiant little soul with a back garden. The front of the cottage had a small patch of garden edging on to the street, but a long garden was out the back, hidden from view. I'd never even seen the house. It wasn't that far from the flat, on the opposite side of the city up a tiny street that time seemed to have forgotten.

The buildings on either side towered above the cottage, offices mainly.

So what was the catch? And what was it doing there?

According to the description it was a single–storey house, a protected building that couldn't be flattened to make way for new structures. The modern world had to build itself around it. And it had.

The photographs showed that it had a bathroom with an old–fashioned bathtub and overhead shower, a kitchen that led to the large back garden with well–cared for flower beds and a lawn. The house itself had one bedroom, and another toilet in the hallway. Just a little loo with a hand wash basin, accessed via a sliding door. A long lounge ran from the front of the house through to the back. Glass doors let in the garden view and opened out on to a small patio.

The kitchen was traditional but beautifully functional. It was shiny and clean yet well–loved. I adored the vintage vibe, unintentional I was sure. Everything seemed authentic. The cooker looked like it had made many a tasty stew and casserole with carrots fresh from the garden. Two jam pans sat beside it. In my world they would be ornaments, but it was obvious they were used to make jam that would simmer away on top of the stove.

I pictured having dinner at the wooden table with its patchwork cushioned chair, and selecting my pots and pans from where they hung gleaming copper and heavy iron on the wall. Floral plates, teacups, saucers and other crockery were displayed on the shelves of the wooden dresser.

The cottage was available for a short–term lease from April until the end of September. April was almost over. Part of the lease had gone. The property had been on the market since March. Why didn't people want it? I read the monthly cost. It was expensive. Out of my budget, but I was curious.

I got on my bike and cycled round to have a look at it.

The night air was crisp and I was glad I'd worn an extra jumper. I actually whizzed past the street; it was narrow and tucked into a niche off one of the main areas.

But there was the cottage, sitting all by itself in the glow of the streetlamps. The offices were empty and everything around it was closed for the night. I peered through the front windows. It was so dark inside I couldn't see the interior, just vague outlines of furniture in the lounge lit by the shadowy light shining through the patio doors.

The longer I looked the more I saw as my eyes became accustomed to the darkness. Yes, there was the sofa, two sofas, comfy chairs, a fireplace, tables, a sideboard and a garden out the back. I could just make out the flower beds with spring flowers and a lawn. The property was tiny, but how much room did I need? I sighed to myself. I did like it, but the lease payments were a bit costly. Still...

I cycled back to the flat, occasionally gazing up at the deep velvety sky. I felt so alone in the city and yet...free for the first time in years.

I went back and emailed the estate agent my details and in the morning they phoned me to chat about the property. The property agent woman was very helpful.

'The owner, a retired lady, wants the house lived in and looked after while she's away on a summer break. She's visiting her sister in Cornwall. The cottage has been on the market for a few weeks. A lot of people have enquired about it but the stipulations on the lease agreement have put them off.'

'What stipulations?' I said.

'There is a substantial reduction in the monthly cost of the lease if you agree to one thing. You have to make the house available to the local sewing bee ladies every Wednesday afternoon from 2:00–4:00 p.m.'

'A sewing bee?'

'You only have to supply the tea. They bring their own home baked cakes. And their sewing. Two sewing machines are kept in the living room, tucked along the far wall on a sewing table and dresser. But most of the sewing is done by hand. It's more a social event. Sewing and chatting over afternoon tea with cakes and scones.'

That sounded fine to me. In fact, I quite liked the thought of joining them for a cuppa. I loved to sew. It was part of my work when I tried out my patterns and designs. The great thing about my new contract was that I could live anywhere. All I had to do was draw the patterns and designs and then email them to the company. So I was free to live wherever I wanted.

We chatted some more and she arranged a viewing for me later that morning.

I stood in the lounge and gazed around. The cottage was gorgeous.

'Obviously having the sewing bee is voluntary, but it's important to the owner, Zinnia, so she's offering a reduction in the rent,' the agent explained. 'From what she's told me, it's a friendly group of women.'

'Does Zinnia run the sewing bee?'

'Yes, her mother started it years ago.' She checked her notes. 'Another woman, Jannet, helps to keep it going. She usually looks after the cottage while Zinnia is away in Cornwall for a few days, but this is an extended visit so Zinnia's nephew suggested she put it on the market for hire. Neither of them wanted the burden put on Jannet for the whole summer. Jannet apparently has her own sewing business and house to tend to. But they wanted the sewing bee to continue during the summer. It certainly helps that you've got an interest in sewing, Morag.'

I nodded thoughtfully.

The cottage was an anomaly. A beautifully maintained, fully furnished niche in the middle of the city, protected by zoning laws from being developed into the taller metropolis that had sprung up around it.

Ordinarily such a property furnished and in this location would have been out of my price bracket, but the reduction for the sewing bee brought it within reach.

I could have a lily pad, a five–month stay in a beautiful home, and maybe even make some friends while I built my pattern design portfolio and tried to make a go of things.

As it was furnished, I wouldn't have the cost of buying items for a new house. Almost everything in the flat belonged to Gavyn. It would be great to be able to move from the flat and get on with things.

By the end of the viewing I decided to take a chance and accepted the lease. The cottage was mine until the end of September.

I thought about leaving Gavyn a note the morning I left. Something along the lines of — Dear Cheating Bastard, goodbye forever. But I didn't. I picked up my bag, locked the front door behind me, posted the keys through the letterbox and didn't glance back.

I got into my car which was packed with eight suitcases. Only three of them contained clothes. The rest had my patterns, artwork and designs in them. The ratio of my life was reflected in those suitcases. I put four on the back seat, three in the boot and had one strapped into the front passenger seat. My sewing machine was jammed behind the seat. There was no room for my bicycle so I'd taken it to the cottage already.

The sun was trying to break through the pale grey clouds as I drove across the city to start my new life.

Butterflies of excitement charged through me. I'd done it. I'd actually left the flat and was going to live in a cottage with a garden for a few months. This would give me time to plan where I wanted to go from there.

I parked nearby and lugged my suitcases and sewing machine into the cottage. When it was all unpacked I sighed with relief. I opened the patio doors. I could unwind here, and get on with creating the designs for the new pattern collections. One collection was almost complete. It had been part of my submission to gain the contract. I had three months to finish the collections. They wanted me to think vintage, floral and include things like my old–fashioned designs and watercolour flowers. I could do this. I was sure of it. I couldn't wait to get settled into the cottage and get started on my work.

Every time Gavyn crossed my mind I pushed him aside. Betrayal left such a void and a bitter taste. I popped a barley sugar sweet into my mouth and forced myself not to dwell on traitorous Gavyn. I had to look ahead. And I did — to the picturesque view of the garden.

I could belong here. I could. I really could.

I stepped out into the back garden. It smelled of fresh grass and flowers. Quite a few flowers were blooming even though summer had yet to fully emerge. The owner knew about gardening. Without being regimented, the flowers were planted to give a colour combination that the artist in me appreciated. There were bluebells, roses, pansies of all sorts of colours from white and velvety purple to the palest lilac and cream. The scent was gorgeous. I wished I could've bottled it and kept it for the days when I needed to feel that the world wasn't against me.

My heart lifted a little. Yes it did.

Chapter Two

A Passion For Sewing

I settled in quite well and felt at home in the cottage. Keeping busy kept my mind off thoughts of Gavyn that ranged from teary moments when I wondered what he was doing and if he was happy with her, to wishing that I'd punched him harder that night before cycling out of his life.

I set up my sewing machine beside the two machines in the lounge. I put mine on a dresser that had room for me to sit there comfortably and plenty of drawers to keep my fabrics, sewing accessories, artwork paper and paints. A table beside the dresser was perfect for sketching patterns and cutting fabrics.

The dresser and table faced the wall near the middle of the long lounge. To my right I could see the garden through the glass doors that led on to the patio. To my left I had a view of the street. Not many people went past the window but I enjoyed watching the well–dressed men in their smart suits arriving for work in the offices that sandwiched the cottage between them.

Across the street were other tall buildings, office blocks with nameless doors that everyone who entered seemed to know about. One evening when they'd all gone home I went over and had a look to see if I could fathom what the offices were. Some were accountancy firms which set alarm bells clanging at the thought that Gavyn might walk past one day. Others were so vague that I'd no idea what they were. I eventually deemed it didn't matter and went back to the cottage to make my dinner.

I loved the kitchen. I'd even started baking again. I baked a lemon drizzle cake and some fruit scones. And as I sat in the kitchen spreading butter on a fresh baked scone, I realised that I didn't feel quite so bad about everything that had happened. I liked the cottage and the garden. I'd had a proper look around the garden and noticed that it had lots of old–fashioned plants and cottage garden classics that gave it a vintage feel. I recognised them because of all the flowers I painted. Wild flowers grew at the far wall but appeared to have been encouraged to stay rather than weeded out. This had created a beautiful little wild flower patch along with pretty pink thrift and daisy fleabane that were perfect for ditsy floral prints. Thrift was such an adorable pink flower. To see it growing in the garden made me want to paint it.

In the mornings I'd get up, make breakfast and eat it outside on the patio where there was a wrought iron table and chairs shielded by a garden umbrella. May had arrived bright and breezy but there was more warmth in the sun. During the afternoons it was quite lovely and I wondered if the sewing bee ladies ever sat outside while they stitched whatever it was they were working on.

Not long now until they arrived. It was Wednesday, mid–day. I'd bought in plenty of milk, sugar, tea and coffee. And baked a chocolate cake and a Victoria sponge in case they expected more than a cuppa from me. I also had a full tin of biscuits on standby. Well, minus a chocolate bourbon and a custard cream.

The cottage was tidy but I'd added vases of fresh flowers with greenery from the garden to give a summery look to the place, and put rose petal soap and clean towels in the loo in the hallway.

I wasn't sure what to expect from them. Although I could sew, and had done since I was a little girl, learning from my mother, I'd never been to a sewing bee. My mum used to sew a lot of my clothes and I loved the individuality of wearing something that no one else had. This still appealed to me. There were few hobbies and interests that I could think of that were so personal and yet could be extremely sociable. Skills were passed on from one woman to another (and to a few men of course) instead of being lost in the passing of time. Patterns today that women had snipped from magazines decades ago were still doing the rounds. Because these women had bothered to cut them out and save them, they continued to be part of fashion and dressmaking. I loved the thought of that. I hoped to be part of that, contributing new designs and continuing the techniques and traditions.

I filled the kettle at around 2:00 p.m., and then I heard the doorbell ring. I went to welcome them in. I wore an apron over my blouse and trousers. I'd made it from one of my own patterns in a bright and cheerful bumblebee fabric.

Three women were on my doorstep. Each of them had a voluminous sewing bag that looked like it had been made in different fabrics from the same pattern. They were also laden with cakes.

'Hello, I'm Jannet. This is Denice and Sharla. You must be Morag.'

'Yes, pleased to meet you. Come on in.'

Jannet was a tall brunette, slim and in her fifties. Denice was slightly younger, forties, and shorter with a penchant for purple. Her jacket, trousers, blouse and bag were in shades of purple and lilac. Sharla looked to be in her late twenties and wore jeans and a top that had an appliqué teacup on it. Her nails were varnished in ice cream pastel colours.

As they stepped inside, a handful of other women came hurrying along the street.

'Are we late?' one of them gasped.

'No,' I assured them. 'I've got the kettle on for the tea.'

When I went into the lounge Jannet and Denice were missing. I found them in the kitchen sorting the cups and saucers, heating two large teapots, boiling the kettle, and setting up the cakes and scones they'd brought for the afternoon tea.

'I wasn't sure how you like things set up,' I said.

'Oh don't you fret, Morag,' said Jannet. 'We're used to organising things.'

Which was definitely the case because when I went through to the lounge carrying two plates piled with slices of Victoria sponge and chocolate cake they'd rearranged the furniture to create the sewing bee. Two tables were put together in the centre so that the tea and cakes could be accessed while they sat on the sofas and chairs with their sewing. All eight of them had sewing bags that looked like they were handmade. I had one too but mine was a totally different design, made from two fat quarters of fabric with vintage prints and lined with light blue satin.

'Are you joining us, Morag?' said Denice, bringing through a tray of cups and saucers and putting it down on one of the tables.

'Eh...well, yes, that would be nice.'

'Of course you're joining us,' said Jannet. She'd put a flowery print tea cosy over one of the large pots of tea. 'We want to hear all about you. Where you're from. What you do. And why you're living here.'

'Now don't you go harassing Morag before she's even had a chance to chat to us, Jannet,' one of the women scolded her.

'I'm not harassing you, am I, Morag?' Jannet's brown eyes peered out from behind her spectacles at me.

'Not at all,' I said, wondering if this was true.

With the afternoon tea made, we all settled down to chat. Sewing bags were at the ready but everyone was staring at me as Jannet began harassing, sorry, asking me about myself.

'What is it you do? I notice that you've got a sewing machine.'

Several of them nodded at me.

'I'm a pattern designer.'

Every teacup rattled in its saucer.

Jannet's eyes blinked in quick succession. 'Patterns? As in...sewing patterns?'

'Yes. I'm an artist and I design patterns that are used for quilt blocks, appliqué and various crafts. I use a lot of my floral artwork to make template designs that are used by women like yourselves to sew into quilts, cushion covers, to decorate an apron pocket, for appliqué or embroidery...'

The cakes and scones sat untouched. A few sipped their tea. Other sat still listening to every word, though I could see from their reaction the one word that fascinated them was — *patterns*.

'And I also make full patterns for items such as a tea dress or a top that can be used as a paper sewing pattern.'

'Sewing patterns?' murmured Sharla.

I nodded.

'Phone Zinnia,' Jannet announced to the ladies. 'Tell her to stay with her sister in Cornwall for the rest of the year. We're keeping Morag. She makes patterns. We're sorted now forever.'

We all started laughing.

'Are we allowed to see any of your new patterns?' said Denice.

I showed them some sketches and a couple of paper patterns that I was working on.

'This is a flower design,' I said. 'It's a Cupid's dart.'

'A what?' said Denice.

'A blue flower with a long spindly stem,' I said. 'I like to make different flowers as well as the popular tea roses and bluebells. I try to create something new. The finished outline of this can be used for sewing.'

'What type of flower is this?' one of them asked picking up one of my designs. 'Is it a real daisy or did you make up the yellow and brown colours?'

The daisy had yellow petals and a brown centre. 'It's a chocolate daisy. A real flower but again, something a bit different.'

'A chocolate daisy?' said Sharla. 'I've never heard of those. Does Zinnia have them in her garden? She's got a lot of old-fashioned flowers and others that I don't recognise.'

'I don't think so, but as I'll be here until September I could plant some. They flower during the summer and they smell of chocolate.'

'I'm definitely including those in my new quilt,' said Jannet. 'When will the patterns be available to buy?'

'I'm designing a couple of new collections for a company.' I explained about my work situation and getting the contract. 'I have to keep the new designs exclusive. However, I have lots of patterns that you're welcome to use. Plenty of flowers and other variations of the chocolate daisy pattern. And I have apron patterns, vintage style, that you might like. But I'd appreciate it if you'd keep them for yourselves, just for the sewing bee.' I rustled through my portfolio for sample designs and gave them lots of things that I was happy for them to use.

Jannet held up a pattern piece. I'd printed it on lightweight white paper. It was something I'd designed just for myself. A basic pattern that I'd used before. 'I like the look of this? What is it?'

'It's a pattern for a sewing machine cover. I was going to make a couple of covers for Zinnia's sewing machines. The dust covers are a bit plain. I thought I'd sew a cottage cover and perhaps a vintage floral.'

A ripple of excitement erupted through the sewing bee.

'Sewing machine covers,' said Jannet. 'That could be one of our next projects. What do you think, ladies?'

The women nodded, keen to include this in their to-do sewing list.

'We've not sewn together since Zinnia went away,' said Denice. 'We're so used to coming here on a Wednesday that we never got round to organising another venue. We kept hoping someone would take on the lease.'

'We'll be planning our sewing this afternoon rather than getting a lot done,' said Jannet. 'Besides, we're always nattering and gossiping while we sew.'

'This chocolate cake is delicious,' Denice commented. 'Did you bake this yourself?'

'Yes,' I said. 'I used to bake quite often but I've been so busy with my designs.' And with Gavyn. 'Now that I'm here I seem to have more time for other things, like baking.'

'I didn't start sewing until I was eighteen,' said Sharla. 'When I broke up with my first boyfriend I wept buckets at my auntie's house so she taught me how to knit. Then I got dumped by another fella and learned how to sew a bag. In the past five years I've been unlucky in love. I always pick rotten losers but I've learned how to sew everything from a soft toy to a dress. I even stuffed a row of robins for Christmas to make a draught excluder.'

Jannet and Sharla went through to the kitchen to make more tea while the cake and scones were consumed.

'Jannet's been sewing for years,' Denice said to me. 'She used to be a seamstress. Now she's got her own wee business, sewing and mending from home. Jannet's husband left her last year. Left her with nothing. She's not heard from him since. He's off gadding about in Edinburgh. So she's had to make a living from her sewing.'

'I'm sorry to hear that,' I said.

'I'm the happiest I've been in years,' said Jannet bringing fresh pots of tea through to the lounge. 'That selfish eejit was useless. I'm a new woman these days.'

'Me too,' said Denice. 'I was shattered a couple of years ago when my husband left me for pastures new, but I've got a wee job in an office that keeps me ticking over. My two sons live in London and have their own lives. You know what young men are like. But I've got the ladies here for company and my sewing.' She smiled at me. 'What about you? Are you married?'

I told them about Gavyn. The whole story including punching him in the street.

'Are you a boxer, Morag?' said Jannet. 'You look wiry and fit.'

'No, I was just blazing mad at him.'

Jannet took a couple of imaginary punches at the air, fighting nothing. Or perhaps she pictured her runaway husband being on the receiving end.

'I've never punched a man in my life,' one of them said. Her silver–spun hair wobbled with indignation. 'I always whack them with a rolling pin or my handbag.'

Another woman agreed. 'I don't like the thought of skinning my knuckles. A slap round the chops is what I use when a man gets out of hand.'

'Men are cheeky bampots,' said Sharla. 'Do you know what one of them said to us as we were hurrying up the street on our way to the sewing bee?'

Everyone stopped to listen.

'One of those snooty architects that works across the road,' Sharla pointed out the window, 'asked us if we were heading for our old–fashioned, sweetie wife knitting and sewing. He was being rotten, so I told him what we'd do to him with size ten knitting needles.'

'Knit his balls together for breakfast,' said Jannet.

'More tea?' I said, realising we'd gone off topic.

I poured the tea and nearly spilt it when I noticed a man peering in the front window. Of all the cheek...

'Oh there's Marck,' Jannet announced. 'He phoned me this morning to ask if the sewing bee was back on. He said he'd drop by.' She stood up. 'Has he contacted you?' she asked me.

'No. I don't even know who he is.' But he was handsome that's for sure. A flurry of soft dark curls fell across his forehead and his eyes seemed to have a sparkle in them, even from this distance. Pale blue or pale green? His face was strong with cheekbones that swept up to those fascinating eyes of his. He was extremely well–dressed in a dark suit, shirt and tie and yet he didn't look like the businessmen from the offices nearby. This man was in a class of his own.

'I'll introduce you,' said Jannet, hurrying me towards the door. 'Take a deep breath, Morag, because you're about to meet Zinnia's nephew.'

I frowned at her. 'Is there a problem with that?'

She nodded. 'He's one of the most gorgeous men in the city. I know you're still upset from your break–up but if there was ever a cure he's standing right outside your front door.'

My heart rate increased and I hadn't even met him. Calm down, I told myself. Don't get caught up in Jannet's obvious adoration for him.

I went to open the door but she pulled me back.

'There's something else you should know about him,' she whispered urgently.

I stared at her.

'He's rich, single, talented, early–thirties, sexy and inclined to flirt with anyone he's interested in.'

'Is that all?'

'No, he's an expert at making men's shirts. He can out–sew all of us. The top stitching on his collars is perfection. But he can't knit.'

'Not perfect then, eh?'

An insistent knock thudded on the door.

We both jumped and Jannet made a grab for me. 'Smile and pretend not to notice how gorgeous he is.'

I nodded and opened the door.

Jannet made the introductions. 'This is Morag. She's renting the cottage. She's just moved in. This is the first afternoon sewing bee since your aunt left.'

He smiled at me.

What. A. Smile.

'Pleased to meet you, Morag. I'm Marck.'

We shook hands and I totally swooned. Yep, that's the only word for it. And I wasn't a swooner. Ever.

'Would you like to come in and join us for tea?' I tried to sound bright but casual.

'Thank you.' He was very tall and had to bend his head down slightly to come through the doorway but once inside the cottage he fitted quite well. The shoulders of his tailored jacket tapered down to a trim torso and I got the impression that he was fit.

I could've heard a pin drop when he walked into the lounge. Then the silence was followed by a flurry of activity as the women tried to encourage him to sit down.

He seemed happier walking down to the patio doors and peering out at the garden.

I opened the patio doors. I suddenly needed air. This was ridiculous. I never reacted like this, but he was totally gorgeous. I just wanted to stare at him. The other women did and he didn't seem to notice. He was too busy now looking at my designs that were scattered on my table.

'Who drew these patterns?' he said, sifting through them.

'Morag,' said Jannet. 'She makes patterns for quilt designs — and *sewing patterns*.'

The intense blue–green eyes focussed on me. 'You're a professional designer?'

I explained about the new contract.

He flicked through my portfolio. 'There's a vintage and classic quality to a lot of your work.'

I smiled at him. 'Vintage is one of the themes I'm working on at the moment.'

'Morag's kindly letting us use some of her designs,' said Jannet. 'The ones that aren't part of her new collections.'

'That's very generous of you,' he said. 'I'll let my aunt know. She'll appreciate having someone who sews living here while she's away. The sewing bee is sort of a family tradition. My aunt and my mother were both brought up to sew by my grandmother who started the sewing bee in this house.'

'I'm certainly pleased to be part of it,' I told him.

Jannet and Denice went to make him fresh tea and a slice of my chocolate cake.

He followed them through to the kitchen and I overheard them relay my circumstances to him.

I pretended to be busy sorting my designs when he wandered back through to the lounge.

'There's a sewing dummy in the laundry cupboard,' he said.

'Don't look at me when you're saying that,' Denice joked with him. She put his tea and cake down on a table while he disappeared into the hallway.

He brought a vintage, cream–coloured wire mannequin through and placed it beside my sewing machine. I loved the look of it. I'd wanted one lately but they were quite expensive and I'd never got round to buying one. Besides, it would've looked out of place in Gavyn's modern flat.

Marck compared the mannequin's build to my figure. 'A perfect fit, I think. Small size ten.'

I blushed as he scrutinised me. I felt self–conscious that he was looking at my figure.

I turned the focus on him. 'I hear that you design men's shirts.'

'Yes. And ties and now I'm considering adding a range of waistcoats.'

'We wish he'd design clothes for us, don't we ladies?' said Jannet. 'We've been trying to persuade him for ages but no joy.'

He smiled at them. 'I did think about designing women's clothes when I started out as a designer years ago, but I never had the passion for it.' He turned to me. 'You'll understand what I mean. As a designer you've got to have a passion for your work. That comes across in your designs. You clearly have a talent and a love for what you do.'

'Yes, I believe you have to be very passionate.'

The women giggled, causing me to blush. 'About the eh...my designs. Your designs.'

Jannet laughed. 'Oh I think there's plenty of passion in this wee house today.'

Indeed there was — and he was standing right next to me.

Chapter Three

Bumblebees & Afternoon Tea

Marck sat down on one of the chintz–covered chairs and enjoyed his tea and cake while the women stared at him.

I busied myself, sifting through my patterns. 'What type of things are you interested in making?' I said to the women, flicking through some of the designs in my portfolio. 'How about something that's quick and easy to make?'

'We'll sew anything that's practical, pretty or a challenge,' said Jannet. 'During the past few weeks we've all finished the things we'd been working on. We often plan what we're going to make so that we can share fabrics and accessories. Mind you, we've all got fabric stashes up to the ceiling, so if you're ever looking for a type of material there's a chance one of us has it lurking in our stash.'

I put two patterns on the desk.

'Is that a bumblebee?' said Jannet, straining to see what the patterns were.

'Yes. A bee and a beehive. Ideal for pincushion patterns, though you could also use them as an appliqué quilt block.' I brought them over and showed them the designs. 'You're welcome to use them.'

Jannet was delighted. 'I love sewing things like this that you can make in an afternoon. I'll have a go at making the bee.'

'I could make that by the time the kettle boils,' said Marck.

Denice stood up. 'A hint for more tea, eh Marck?' She went through to make him a fresh cuppa.

He shrugged his broad shoulders. 'I'm just saying that the pincushion seems so easy.'

'It may look easy,' said Jannet, 'but I've made lots of pincushions in my time and designs like this can be fiddly to sew.'

He scoffed.

'I know men's shirts are one of the most difficult items to tailor,' Jannet told him. 'But I'd like to see you make a bumblebee pincushion.'

The other women agreed.

'Be careful, ladies, I might just take you up on your challenge.'

'Fight, fight, fight,' Sharla chanted and fist–pumped the air so hard one of her vanilla–coloured nails popped off.

'You'll take someone's eye out with those,' he said. 'And you'd never be able to punch with those talons.'

'Morag packs quite a punch,' Jannet warned him. 'She panned her ex–boyfriend in the street outside a restaurant recently.'

'Brawling in public is hardly ladylike behaviour,' he said.

'And a comment like that would never come from the mouth of a gentleman,' I said. 'Though perhaps the challenge of sewing a bumblebee has got you on the defensive.'

'Okay, I'll take you up on the challenge, Morag.' He took his jacket off to reveal the full splendour of his taupe shirt that was tailored to perfection.

The competitive side of my nature refused to back down.

He frowned at the little bumblebee design. 'However, I'm not sure where the challenge is in this.'

'It'll test your fiddly–skill ability,' I told him. 'And to work fast under pressure.'

'I'm used to both. I have very demanding customers.'

'You should win then, shouldn't you?' I handed him a bumblebee pattern. Several small pieces. Fiddly but effective. I held up a sketch of the finished product — a pincushion with an appliqué bee.

He looked at it as if it was a project that was beneath his capabilities. 'Are there any other parts to it?'

'No, all the pattern pieces are there. I'll use a rough copy. You can add other little touches for his face — give him eyes and a smile.'

He laughed. 'You're kidding me.'

I shook my head. 'We'll sew it on the clock. A fifteen minute finishing line.'

His sexy lips curved into a smirk. 'I could sew this in five.'

'I'll time you,' said Jannet.

He sat down at one of the machines. 'Doesn't this machine have an automatic needle threader?'

I sat at my machine. 'No, but mine does. You can use it if you can't see where to stick your thread.'

'I can manage. But where's the fabric? Don't start timing us until we've got the fabric ready.'

I pointed to a pile of fabric pieces on the dresser. 'Help yourself. I suggest you avoid the silk. It's difficult to create the right effect with silk. Cotton and velvet work better.'

He deliberately chose two contrasting pieces of silk. One black and one turquoise. 'I'll make it work. Is it okay if I make a blue striped bumble?'

'Whatever you want,' I told him. I chose chocolate brown and amber–yellow cotton. 'There's also a bag of lightweight filler you can use to stuff your bumble.'

I grabbed a large handful of the filler and put it behind my machine ready to stuff the pincushion. Marck did the same.

'Sewing machines and patterns at the ready?' said Jannet.

We both nodded and gave each other a glance as the clock started ticking.

'Go,' shouted Jannet.

I started to cut out my fabric pieces. I heard Marck snipping like crazy but kept my eye on my cutting lines so that I didn't skimp on the seam allowance that was included in the pattern.

We both put our scissors down at the same time. A draw so far. Now for the sewing. I'd made the bumble before, having tried to design several versions until I'd settled on this one.

I glanced at Marck. His capable fingers fed the fabric through the sewing machine. I noticed that he was wearing gold cufflinks. A very classy design — ship's wheels. I wondered if he was into sailing.

'They were a gift from a customer who owns a marina. He was pleased with the shirts and ties I made for him so he gave me these for Christmas.'

Damn, he'd seen me staring at them.

'I thought perhaps sailing was a leisurely pursuit of yours.'

'I don't have time for leisure. My life is one continuous work schedule mixed with crazy interludes like this one. When I came here today I never thought I'd be vying against an attractive and talented blonde to sew a little bumblebee. I do like your bumble by the way.' He threw me a wicked grin.

I tried not to laugh. 'I think you're attempting to distract me so that I'll make a mistake with these seams.'

'My cunning plan is foiled. I guess I'll just have to beat you fair and square.'

I trimmed my seams after sewing them like blazes and then turned the pincushion the right sides out. A small gap was left open for stuffing. I stuffed the filler in, threaded a needle and prepared to sew the gap shut using a ladder stitch.

'A ladder stitch, eh?' he said. 'I kept my gap on the underside and thought I'd stitch it rough and then stick a fabric flower on it. I see you've got a few of those lying around. Mind if I use one?'

'Not at all.' I hurried up with the ladder stitch, closed the gap and then set about sewing the eyes. I snatched two small beads from a tin of bits and bobs and used those. Now for the smile.

'Five minutes left,' Morag told us.

'Come on Morag,' shouted Denice.

Thankfully, the women were backing me. I thought they'd have had the buntings out for Mr Handsome.

For some reason Marck decided to attempt to sew a centre piece on the flower and managed to snag the thread on the sewing machine. Maybe the machine was temperamental. Mine had its little foibles that I worked around. Obviously he wasn't used to the machine and perhaps was a bit heavy handed with it.

He muttered a few choice words and had to use a ripper to unpick the stitches before sewing the flower pieces again. But by that time I'd sat my bumble on the desk and announced, 'Finished.'

A cheer went up.

Marck threw his bumblebee aside. 'I suppose I owe you dinner, Morag.'

'Dinner?'

The women muttered and nudged each other.

'I think you've won more than the bumblebee challenge,' Jannet said to me, causing me to blush as pink as the flower that hadn't quite made its way on to Marck's pincushion.

'You don't have to buy me dinner, Marck. It was just a little bit of fun.'

'I bet that's what he's got in mind for after dinner,' said Sharla.

'You're right,' said Marck. 'My intentions are completely dishonourable.'

Before I could decide whether or not I was flattered, I saw a man climbing over the garden wall. He wore tight jeans and a check shirt with the sleeves rolled up to the elbows. He jumped down and seemed accustomed to entering by this method for his boots missed trampling on any of the flowers. He pushed his tangle of thick, straight blond hair back from his face to reveal a handsome profile that went well with his tall, lean–hipped and long–legged physique. I reckoned he was in his early thirties.

Like a needle pointing north, the women's attention swung from Marck to the intruder. I can't say I blamed them. Tall, dark and handsome versus rugged, golden–haired and sexy. Tough choice.

Marck's expression fell.

No one was perturbed that the man was now opening the shed door and trailing out an ancient lawnmower, one of those push mowers.

'Ruary's lovely, isn't he?' Jannet said to me. 'He comes once a fortnight to sort out your garden.'

'Zinnia has a gardener?' The estate agent hadn't mentioned this to me.

'Yes,' said Marck. 'My aunt hired Ruary when the garden got too much for her to deal with on her own.'

'He's a vintage gardener,' said Jannet. 'Specialises in old–fashioned flowers and plants that my gran used to have in her garden when I was a girl.'

'That explains why there are so many classic flowers,' I said.

'So he's all yours for the summer,' said Jannet.

Oh, if only.

'I'll introduce you.' Marck sounded unenthusiastic but duty–bound to take me out to meet the gardener.

'Ruary,' Marck called to him. 'Come and meet, Morag. She's taken the lease for the summer.'

Ruary glanced round and then came over, brushing his hands down his jeans before shaking my hand and smiling at me.

'Would you like to come in for a cup of tea and a slice of cake?' I offered.

'Ruary doesn't come inside the cottage, do you?' said Marck.

Ruary gave me an intriguing smile. 'Not usually, but I could be tempted today.'

Marck glared at him and forced a grin. 'In that case, I can thoroughly recommend a slice of Morag's chocolate cake. I don't know what she puts in it, but it's delicious.'

'What do you put in it?' said Ruary as we headed inside.

'I eh...I add chocolate liqueur and whisky to the ganache to give some kick to the flavour.'

'Ganache?' The blue eyes focussed on me. 'Is that the topping?'

'Yes, the smooth chocolate coating on the cake. And I add a dash of liqueur to the cream sometimes, depending on how lavish I want it to be.'

'The more lavish the better,' said Ruary.

When the women saw that Ruary was joining them a flurry of excited chair shuffling began as they made room for the handsome gardener in their midst.

Ruary took his heavy boots off and left them on the patio before stepping inside the living room. Unfortunately one of his socks had a large hole in the big toe.

'Oh, you've got a potato,' Denice announced, and then insisted on sorting it for him.

Despite mild protestation from Ruary, he was overpowered by the women and before he'd even had a chance to sip his tea they had him sitting on the sofa with his feet up while Denice took a needle and thread and began mending his sock.

'You just missed seeing Morag beat Marck at a wee sewing challenge,' Jannet told him. 'She sewed a bumblebee pincushion faster than he could manage.'

Ruary grinned over at Marck. 'I bet that stung.'

'I'll never live it down. The ladies obviously won't let me forget it.'

'So you're a sewist then, like Zinnia?' Ruary said to me.

'Morag designs patterns. *Sewing patterns*,' Jannet said before I could respond. 'She paints flowers and creates then into designs. I'm going to be making a chocolate daisy quilt.'

'Chocolate daisy. Berlandiera lyrata.' Ruary murmured the botanical name. His deep voice sounded so sexy.

'You know it?' I said.

He nodded. 'There used to be some in the garden.'

'I was going to plant a few. I wasn't sure if Zinnia had them.'

'I'll sort that out for you. I'll bring them with me the next time I'm here. I've got them in my garden at home.'

Denice finished mending Ruary's sock. 'Thanks, Denice.' He picked up his chocolate cake.

'Morag says the daisies smell of chocolate,' said Sharla.

Ruary smiled. 'They do, but they don't smell as delicious as Morag's chocolate cake.'

A van stopped outside the cottage and two men got out.

'I think you've got more visitors,' one of the women near the window called over to me.

'Does it usually get so busy on a Wednesday?' I said.

'No,' said Marck. 'Ruary's usually in the garden, I'm not here and it's just the sewing bee ladies.'

Ruary got up, taking the less than subtle hint from Marck, but Jannet insisted he have another cup of tea.

I went to answer the door.

'Thank goodness you're in,' one of the men said. 'We've been here the past few Wednesdays trying to get an answer but no one has been home.' He was in his late thirties, well–spoken with quite a pleasant voice. The other man had camera equipment with him and was trying to peer inside the cottage.

'Can I help you?' I said.

'We're filming a television news piece. I'm Craig and I've brought a cameraman with me. We're putting together a piece on the increase in popularity of sewing. The sales of sewing machines have soared during the past few months and sewing classes are inundated with people wanting to learn. We were hoping to include this sewing bee as it's probably the oldest in the city. It's certainly one of the most unusual locations. The cottage has the look we're after for the programme. Would you be interested in saying a few words on camera and letting us film inside the cottage? We were given the owner's name. Zinnia.'

By now Jannet and Marck were in the hall behind me.

'I'm Zinnia's nephew, Marck.'

I let Marck decide whether he wanted the cottage to be part of whatever the television news feature was.

Marck asked a few questions and they chatted about what would be included.

Jannet and I listened. Craig explained that they'd filmed all the other footage and had hoped to get the final shots of the sewing bee in the cottage. They belonged to one of the main media companies and everything seemed to be above board. Marck asked me if I was happy to be part of it. I saw no reason why not.

We brought the interviewer and cameraman into the cottage and introduced them to the women who were extremely excited to be filmed.

'Do you sew?' Craig asked Marck. 'We're keen to include men in the shots. We've only got a few.'

Marck explained about being a shirt designer and that he could indeed sew.

'And what about you?' Craig said to Ruary.

'I'm just the gardener.'

'Would you be interested in perhaps filling in and looking as if you're part of the ladies sewing bee. Two handsome guys would really give us a great angle on this.'

Ruary shrugged his broad shoulders. 'I suppose so.'

That was all the encouragement Craig needed. Another man emerged from the van with lighting and it was set up quickly while Marck and Ruary sat in front of a sewing machine each.

They asked me to sit at my machine and look like I was busy sewing, so I used some vintage afternoon tea material that I planned to make into a sewing machine cover.

Marck showed his skills by feeding two pieces of silk through his machine, while Ruary pretended to know what he was doing with a teacup print pattern that I'd designed for quilt blocks.

'What am I supposed to be sewing?' Ruary whispered to me.

'A tea quilt. All the blocks, the squares, are made individually and then sewn together to make a quilt.'

'I wouldn't mind one of these,' Ruary said, admiring the pattern. 'I like the colours — browns, blues, golds. I could live with these colours.'

The women had been instructed to sew as if they weren't being filmed, so more tea and cake was put out on the tables to create the sewing bee atmosphere.

Around fifteen minutes of footage was filmed. Shots were taken from various angles, including close–ups at the sewing machines. Jannet's needlework was included and she demonstrated her hand sewing prowess.

Marck used his shirt–making skills to full effect by expertly feeding a classic stripe fabric through his sewing machine with the speed and accuracy of a master.

'We want to have a few shots of paper patterns being cut,' said Craig. 'Could you use some of your patterns, Morag?'

'Would this apron pattern suffice?' I held up the paper pattern pieces that I'd drawn.

'That would be great,' he said, and they filmed close–ups of me cutting around the pattern pieces, pinning them to a floral cotton fabric and then cutting out the fabric pieces to make the apron.

I then moved on to stuffing a robin that I'd been working on. The fabric pieces for the robin were already sewn together. I stuffed the softie with lightweight filler, the type used to fill soft toys, and then stitched up the gap. This was included in the filming. Craig wanted all sorts of items featured to show the range of things that were made at the sewing bee.

'Can we take some shots of the garden?' said Craig. The sun was out and the garden looked lovely and he wanted to include the back view of the cottage.

I was beckoned outside. 'I'll chat to you while we walk from the garden back into the lounge,' Craig explained to me. 'We'll walk at a slow pace. Tell me about the sewing bee, about any of the projects you're working on.'

I looked a little nervous.

'Don't worry,' said Craig. 'We'll edit out anything we don't need. Just chat as if we're friends and you're explaining to me about the popularity of sewing. So let's start, Morag...what is it that's made sewing so popular these days? It seems to be enjoying a revival with all sorts of people becoming involved.'

'I think that people are realising it's a great way to make clothes or other items for themselves, their families or as gifts for friends. I've also noticed that when money is tight, a make do and mend attitude seems to thrive and there's no better way to save money and make new things than home sewing.'

'Would you say that this is perhaps linked to the popularity of vintage clothes and increased trends for retro and classic fashions for the home?' said Craig.

'Yes, definitely. Vintage has been a big influence on sewing and crafts, and I think the friendships that are formed in the sewing bees are equally important.'

'Home baking seems to be another part of the whole dynamic. Would you agree, Morag?'

'I would. Home baking, sewing, knitting and all sorts of crafts have become extremely fashionable. Things that were quaint or had an old–fashioned reputation are now enjoyed by a new generation of sewists. And others have found a renewed interest in sewing that they haven't done in years.'

'Is this part of your work or is it a hobby interest?'

'I'm a pattern designer, so it's part of my work. I'm living in the cottage throughout the summer and the sewing bee is held every Wednesday. The ladies and the eh...the men...are planning on making various things — everything from dresses to quilts. There's something for everyone.'

By now we'd stepped inside the cottage and Craig turned his questions to Marck.

'So, Marck, you're a designer of men's shirts. When did your interest in sewing begin?'

Marck explained about learning to sew from his mother, his aunt and his gran.

'And have you any plans to include a fashion show of some of the things you're making here?'

'I have a fashion show every season but it would be great to include some of the things from the sewing bee as part of the show. Maybe we'll do that.'

Jannet looked at me and mouthed — *fashion show?*

'Let us know if you go ahead with that,' said Craig. 'We could use it as a follow–up to the feature.'

The filming concluded with more shots of the cottage and the women sewing.

'When is this going to air?' said Marck.

'We've already got everything else ready, so once this section is edited, it'll go out on the morning news as an interest piece early on Friday.

'As soon as that?' I said.

'This was a last minute chance that we could include the old cottage. We'll edit this tonight and tomorrow and then it'll go out on air.'

'How exciting,' said Jannet.

The women were chattering and everyone was buzzing with the thought of being on television.

After the media people left, Marck said, 'Remember, don't be disappointed if this is cut to a *blink and you'll miss us* snippet.'

We all agreed not to get carried away. I thought it was likely that we'd get a mention in the news feature but it wasn't a sure thing. When the footage was edited most of what had been filmed might never be seen.

'At least it was exciting to be included,' I said. 'It could give a boost to the sewing bee. You never know what something like this could lead to. More women might want to join, and I'm sure we can make room for them.'

'Exactly,' Jannet agreed. 'And it would be lovely to see wee bits of our sewing on the television. Wouldn't that be great?'

Chapter Four

Chocolate Daisies

Jannet was the last to leave. Marck left with the media guys who wanted to film how men's shirts were tailored. Marck had a shop in the city that included a workroom where the shirts were made.

The ladies cleared up everything, washed the teacups, tidied the kitchen and put the living room back the way it was before they'd arrived.

'We never leave any mess for you to clear up,' Jannet explained.

We sat in the kitchen and had a cup of tea.

'Did Marck arrange that dinner date?' she asked.

'No, I don't think he was serious about us having dinner.'

'I wouldn't be too sure about that, Morag. Marck's quite a flirt with the ladies and I saw a wee spark of interest when he looked at you.'

I sipped my tea. 'He was just being friendly.'

'I like Marck, but in truth, he's a bit of a snooty–nose.'

I laughed.

'It's true,' she insisted. 'It's how he was brought up. The family has always had money and Marck's made a success of his own business. He's quite a catch if you're okay about doing as you're told.'

'I'm not okay about that. My ex used to complain about it.'

'He wasn't the man for you then.'

'No, I suppose not.'

She looked thoughtful. 'Ruary seems quite taken with you.'

I felt the colour rise in my cheeks.

'Oh, so Ruary's the one you're interested in?'

'I didn't say that.'

'No, but your face tells quite a story, Morag.'

I smiled and concentrated on my tea.

'Come on,' she urged me. 'What do you think of Ruary? A handsome one, isn't he?'

'He's handsome, but...'

'But what?'

I shrugged. 'I've just come out of a rotten break–up.'

'All the more reason to let your hair down and have a bit of fun.'

Is that what Ruary was? A bit of fun?

'I think I'll take some time out from romance, enjoy the summer here at the cottage, then think about getting back into the dating fiasco.'

'It is a fiasco, isn't it?' she mused. 'I'm resigned to being on my own these days.'

'You'll meet someone new though. It just takes time.'

The brown eyes peered at me through her glasses. 'Maybe I will, maybe I won't. Denice is the same as me. We're not back out there on the dating scene. We tried once, one night, to have a girls' night out with some of the other ladies from the bee.' She giggled. 'What a night. It was at Christmas and we thought we'd get dressed up and hit the town.'

'What happened? And did it involve snogging?'

'Snogging? More like getting our arses felt. There was no finesse, no romance. It was probably the time of year but the men we met were only interested in a fancy fling for the night. We weren't interested.'

'What did you do?'

'We ended up buying fish suppers and going home to my house and getting sozzled on my home–made ginger wine.'

'You must give me the recipe.'

'I'll bring a bottle next Wednesday. Sip it slowly. It's potent stuff. And speaking of potent stuff...Ruary's climbing over the garden wall again.' She got up. 'I'll leave you to it.'

'No, Jannet. Don't go.'

She was already picking up her sewing bag. 'I'll see you next week. You have my number if you need anything. And I'd really like to get that chocolate daisy pattern started for a quilt.'

I gave her a rough copy of one of the quilt block patterns. 'Take this.'

'Thanks, Morag. You're very kind.' She scurried through the living room, glancing at Ruary who was heading towards the patio.

'Phone and let me know if lover boy makes a date with you,' she whispered.

'Don't be silly. He's probably just here with more flowers for the garden.'

She gave me a look. 'That's what you think.'

I waved her off at the front door and then went through to the living room. Ruary was standing on the patio. He smiled when he saw me.

'I wondered if you'd like to choose some plants for the garden?' he said. 'I've got a few that would be perfect for your work. I thought it would be better if you chose what you'd like rather than let me pick them.'

'You're the vintage garden expert. I'd be happy with whatever you select.'

He smiled but his expression had a hidden undertone. Had I scuppered his intentions?

'I've got a large garden. I thought maybe...with you being interested in painting flowers, that you'd like to visit and see the plants for yourself. You're welcome to photograph any you need for your artwork. The garden's looking lovely just now. May is always a great month for the first flush of summer flowers.'

Okay, so he was luring me to visit his garden, and I sensed a little bit of flirting going on. Not that I was complaining. My heart fluttered quicker than it had in ages. Ruary was a very attractive man.

'I was hoping to tempt you,' he said and then corrected himself. 'What I mean is...tempt you to see the flowers while they're at their height. My house is on the outskirts of the city.'

I pictured a rambling house with a large garden that smelled gorgeous and was filled with vintage flowers, bumblebees and butterflies. Somehow my mind put together a scenario of sitting in the early evening sun, sipping tea and chatting to Ruary about his flowers. I went to refuse his offer from habit, so used to being with Gavyn, then I realised that there was no reason to say no.

'Yes,' I heard myself say, and saw the smile light up his rugged features before I could withdraw my acceptance feeling suddenly vulnerable. Was this a date or just a friendly invitation? I was about to find out.

We drove in his car through the city centre and then towards the outskirts where Ruary lived. A mellow glow from the sun filtered through the windscreen. It was teatime and the traffic was busy as people headed home from work.

'Why do you climb over the garden wall?' I asked him.

'Habit. With the cottage being sandwiched between the offices it's the easiest access, especially when Zinnia is away. There's a road at the back of the cottage and I hop over the wall when I need in.'

'Is Zinnia away often?'

'She visits her sister in Cornwall regularly. They're both experts themselves when it comes to flowers, but I help Zinnia with the heavy work in the garden, cutting the grass and so forth.'

'Have you always been a gardener?'

'Yes. I come from a family of gardeners. My grandfather had a market garden and I was brought up learning how to grow tomatoes and vegetables and then I concentrated on vintage flowers. His garden had a vast selection of old–time flowers that some gardens have long since lost. But there's more interest in vintage plants these days. You'll know that yourself from your designs. You mentioned that your new collections have a vintage theme.'

'They do. And they work well as fabric prints.'

'I grow the flowers, you paint them and make them into patterns, and the sewing bee women sew them into garments. We all have our place in keeping the old–fashioned traditions going.'

I nodded, and then admired the handsome profile as he drove through the city. His lashes were quite dark and emphasised his blue eyes. His features were strong, his jaw firm, giving him a determined look.

We drove through an upmarket area where there were numerous houses on tree–lined streets. Large houses with equally large gardens. At the far end a mansion sat back in the road, partially hidden by the trees that gave it a beautiful seclusion.

Ruary drove up the long driveway.

'This is your house?' I didn't manage to hide the admiration in my tone. I would've loved to own a house like this. I loved the cottage, but this...this was in a league of its own. The house was huge. Well–cared for and yet with an old world charm. The garden surrounded it, blending perfectly, creating a setting that made me want to sigh as we drove up and parked outside the front entrance.

'It used to belong to my grandparents. I inherited it.'

'It's gorgeous.'

'The house is far too large for a single man but I wouldn't ever want to live anywhere else. I love the garden. It's ideal for my work.'

He led the way inside the mansion. Dark wood flooring and expensive rugs in burgundy and gold tones gave the decor a traditional feel. We went through the lounge with its massive fireplace, unlit of course, and into the kitchen which was probably as big as Zinnia's entire cottage. He opened the kitchen's patio doors and the scent of the flowers from the garden poured in, filling the air with their fresh fragrance.

The kitchen was tidy, well–kept. I suspected that he had a cleaner or someone who came in to keep the house looking clean but homely.

'Sometimes I rent part of the house. There's even a kitchenette in that part so anyone who lives there has their own cooking facility and I have my privacy. But there's no one renting it at the moment. I'm on my own just now. I hope you'll stay for dinner.'

'Dinner? I wouldn't want to put you to any bother.'

'Nothing fancy. I'll pick some vegetables from the garden and there's fish in the freezer if that's fine with you?'

My mouth watered at the thought of vegetables fresh from the garden. Embarrassingly, my tummy rumbled. 'Sorry, I've been so busy, I haven't eaten anything accept cake today and a couple of biscuits.'

Ruary rolled up his shirt sleeves to reveal the corded muscles of his forearms. He had a really lean and fit physique. I tried not to think about him like that. It was too distracting and I genuinely wanted to see the flowers and plants he had. I followed him out of the kitchen into the back garden. A path led to a vegetable patch. When I say patch, this patch was extensive.

'What type of veg would you like, Morag? The lettuce are looking good, and I've got spring onions, carrots and potatoes.'

'All of those sound delicious. We could have boiled potatoes and carrots with the fish and a side salad. I'll help with the cooking if you want.'

'Two sets of hands make lighter work.' He pulled a leafy lettuce, shook the soil from it and put it in a basket. Then he gathered the other vegetables we'd chosen. He also picked a couple of large tomatoes from his greenhouse — one red and a sweet golden yellow.

We took them inside and I started to wash them while he got the fish from the freezer — Scottish salmon fillets. He reached up into one of the cupboards. 'I've got packets of sauce that would go nicely with this.' We chose a savoury white sauce with parsley.

While the potatoes and carrots boiled, I chopped the spring onions and prepared the lettuce and tomatoes.

'It's been a long time since I've had company for dinner,' he said, setting the kitchen table with plates and cutlery. Even the plates were vintage and the cutlery was an old, heavy, traditional type that makes eating a meal feel extra special.

Ruary cooked the fish while I dealt with the veg.

I glanced at him a few times, working away quite skilfully preparing the fish and arranging the bread and little extras for the meal. I almost had to pinch myself. I'd expected a busy time with the sewing bee. However, I hadn't thought that I'd be cooking dinner with a handsome man, a vintage gardener.

My heart beat faster as I admired his physique, and when he reached across to pick up the sea salt, his tall, manly presence caused all sorts of reactions deep inside me. But I still felt comfortable in his company. This was something I hadn't experienced in a long time. Gavyn took no interest in cooking our food. He preferred to eat out often or sit himself down and wait for me to rustle up our meals. I didn't mind, but it was nice to share the cooking chores with a man who seemed happy and content to make dinner.

He caught me staring at him. I looked away and chopped the spring onions.

'This must seem strange for you,' he said.

I nodded.

'I assure you that you can relax around me. I'm not like Marck.'

'Do you know him well?'

He turned the sizzling salmon over in the pan and continued to cook at the stove. 'We've known each other for a long time. Our paths have crossed since we were in our teens. Our families moved in the same circles.'

'Jannet says that Marck comes from an affluent background.'

'His family have money, and he inherited some of it and built his own wealth through his business. But my family were well off too. I'm not trying to impress you. Just explaining how we know each other. His grandmother used to buy flowers from us, and then Zinnia and her sister did too, until her sister married and moved to live with her husband in Cornwall.'

'I'd like to visit Cornwall. It looks lovely with fresh sea air and the little towns and seaside villages.'

'I love Cornwall, but I love Scotland too, the big cities like Glasgow and Edinburgh, the Ayrshire coast and the highlands. I'm lucky because I travel throughout the year to various flower shows and events. I visit Cornwall a few times every year.'

'Lucky you.'

'Glasgow is beautiful though,' he said.

'Yes, it is, and Zinnia's cottage is so lovely. When I was looking for somewhere to live I couldn't believe that there was a house like that in the city centre. I'd gone online to find a house with a garden. I'd been living in a flat and when I split up with my boyfriend it was a chance for a fresh start. I'd always wanted to live in a house with a garden.'

He looked at me as if he was sorry for the years that I'd missed out on the joy of stepping out into a garden, and for the first time in ages, I felt sorry for myself.

'You're welcome to drop by and enjoy the garden here whenever you want. When Zinnia comes back, I assume you'll move somewhere else in the city.'

'Yes. Hopefully somewhere that has a garden, though I'll probably end up in a flat again. I've no plans to leave the city and houses like Zinnia's are few and far between.'

'What about living in a house like this?'

I guffawed. 'I could never afford this type of house.'

'You could live in the rented part. I don't charge extortionate rates.'

'Live here?'

He shrugged. 'Why not? When Zinnia comes back, this would give you somewhere else to move to without leaving Glasgow. It would certainly save me looking for a new renter. I'm fussy about who I share the house with. Some people would ruin the garden and want wild, all–night parties.'

'I'm not really the wild, party type.'

'No fun, huh?' he teased.

I threw a piece of spring onion at him and he caught it easily.

We continued to chat about his gardening work while we cooked the dinner and then we sat down to enjoy it.

'This is delicious,' I said, savouring the salmon topped with the sauce. There was nothing quite like vegetables straight from the garden. The potatoes tasted superb. I'd have happily eaten them, topped with a knob of butter and sprinkled with spring onions, as a meal in themselves.

'Thanks for helping to make it.'

I smiled at him across the table, remembering the last time I'd had dinner with Gavyn. He'd barely said a word to me and ate his meal while continuing to check his phone for text messages.

As I thought about this, the phone rang in the lounge. I expected Ruary would hurry through to answer it. That's what Gavyn would've done. No, correction. Gavyn's mobile was a permanent fixture of himself. He'd have taken the call while eating his meal and had done on numerous occasions even though he knew I hated it.

The phone continued to ring, a pale resonance in the background.

'I don't mind if you want to answer it,' I said. I thought I should make the offer.

He shook his head. 'We're having dinner. They can leave a message.'

The phone stopped ringing.

Ruary didn't even mention it. Instead he asked about my designs — and about Gavyn.

'We split up last month. I caught him cheating on me. I was living with him at his flat in Glasgow and had to move out. I saw Zinnia's cottage advertised and took a chance on it. It's ideal for working on my designs. The flowers in her garden are particularly useful.'

'If you need any other flowers let me know. There's every chance that I have them in my garden or know someone who grows them.'

'I noticed that you have teasel and sweet peas. I brought my camera. Would you mind if I snapped photographs of the flowers to use for my artwork?'

'Not at all. There are plenty of blooms around the other side of the house. I'll show you after dinner. You can pick any you want to take back with you.'

After dinner, I went to clear the dishes.

'Leave them. I'll put them in the dishwasher. Get your camera ready. We'll go outside while the sun's still got some warmth in it.'

I got my camera from my bag while Ruary rattled around in the kitchen, clearing the table, and then we headed outside.

The air was scented with flowers and the woody aroma of the trees. There were apple and pear trees and a row of cherry trees. We walked along the narrow paths that were edged with flowers and plants. Occasionally there was a feature such as a tiny pond, and the garden solar lights had started to flicker.

I photographed several flowers that I knew I was going to use as part of my designs including sweet peas and love–in–a–mist.

We stopped at the chocolate daisies. The delicious chocolate scent wafted through the early evening air, mingling with the fragrance from the sweet peas.

I took snaps of the chocolate daisies, even though I had sketches of them, because they were flowering so beautifully in Ruary's garden.

'I'll plant a few of these in Zinnia's garden the next time I'm over there,' he promised. 'You'd better have one of those chocolate cakes of yours ready because when the women smell the cocoa fragrance they'll be lusting after chocolate.'

And lusting after him.

'I'll make sure I have extra chocolate cake on standby.'

'And perhaps a slice for the gardener?'

'Definitely a slice for you.'

He smiled at me and I wondered why he lived alone. So I asked him in the same straightforward way he'd asked me about Gavyn. 'Is there a reason why you live here all alone? Is it by choice or circumstances?'

'Ruddy rotten choices when it comes to dating. I've hardly ever found any woman that was happy to fit in with my work. And any that have...well...I wasn't attracted to them enough. I think that friendship matters in a relationship. I'd like a wife who was my best friend, but I also believe you've got to have real passion for each other. I did date someone last summer but the spark faded very quickly. She lives in Edinburgh now and we don't keep in contact.' He smiled and looked particularly boyish as he admitted, 'I suppose I'm looking for a woman who makes me want to lift her up and carry her through to the bedroom for a night of passion on a regular basis.'

I blushed and tried not to think about him doing this with me.

As the solar lights glowed in the twilight, I reluctantly went back into the kitchen. 'Thanks for dinner, Ruary, and for the flowers.' He'd picked a basket full, enough to fill two or three vases. The cottage was going to smell wonderful.

'Would you like a cup of tea before I drive you back?'

'There's no need. I'll take a taxi.'

He wouldn't hear of it, and insisted we have tea before he drove me back.

I wandered through to the lounge while he brewed a pot of tea. I looked at the fireplace and pictured it lit up on cold winter nights. He saw me gazing at it as he brought the tea through.

'Have you lit the fire in the cottage yet?' he asked, handing me a cup of tea.

'No. I should do though. Enjoy the whole cottage experience.'

'There is a supply of logs behind the shed in your garden. They give off a great aroma of pine. They're left over from Christmas.'

I wondered whether or not to admit that I'd never actually lit a fire before and wasn't sure what to do. Rather than ask I thought I'd find methods online. I'd never done things like this, such simple things, like creating a real log fire.

I tried to take in how the logs and firelighters were stacked in the fireplace.

'Do you know how to light a fire? How to set it up?' he asked.

I shook my head.

'It's easy,' he said, and proceeded to show me the basics.

I suddenly felt sad...sad for all the homely things that I'd missed out on, things that Ruary and Zinnia took for granted. Or did they? Ruary seemed to appreciate everything he had.

'If you do decide to come and live with me, you know...to rent part of the house...you'll pick up all the little things that make living here a pleasure.'

Including seeing Ruary's handsome face in the mornings? Or was that an added extra that didn't come with the lease?

Chapter Five

Fashion, Fabric & Flirting

Ruary drove me back to the cottage. I waved him off and carried the basket of cut flowers he'd given me inside.

I'd just finished arranging them into vases when Marck knocked on the front door.

'I've been phoning the cottage but got no reply,' he said sounding slightly harassed.

I invited him in.

'I was having dinner at Ruary's house. He gave me flowers from his garden to use for my artwork.'

Marck looked at the extra vases of flowers in the living room. The scent from the flowers I'd added earlier for the sewing bee mingled with the sweet peas, chocolate daisies and other flowers that Ruary had given me. Marck made no comment but his expression showed a hint of...what? Jealousy perhaps? Or that his nose was out of joint that I'd had dinner with Ruary?

'It would be handy if I had your mobile number so that I can contact you if you're...dining out.'

I gave him my number. 'What was it you wanted? Has something happened?'

'Yes. When I got back to my studio there was a message from one of my buyers. They're interested in my new line of men's waistcoats. They already buy my shirts for some of the main suppliers. Now they're interested in the waistcoats. They want me to push ahead with the finished designs and I haven't decided on the fabric print for the back of the waistcoats. The fabric will be silk–based. I don't want it to be plain. I want a hint of a pattern. Nothing too noticeable, just enough to give a feeling of quality and interest to the fabric. I thought I had another month to decide on this, and I have a fabric printer who makes up the material I need at short notice. However, I haven't actually got the finished design, and I was wondering...if you could come up with something to help me out.'

'A fabric design for the back of the men's waistcoats?' I clarified.

'Yes. Could you design a print for me? I need it pretty damn quick.'

'I suppose I could. I'd need to see your waistcoats to come up with an idea of what would be suitable.'

He seemed happy with this and more or less bundled me out of the house, into his car and drove to his shop that was situated in the city centre. His studio was at the back of the shop — a room filled with menswear fabric for suits and shirt fabrics. Shelves were piled with a fantastic selection of classic wool and worsted materials. There was everything from plain greys, neutrals and navy colours to pinstripes and plaids. The shirt fabrics were predominantly cotton and linen in neutral tones and blues.

Marck flicked the main lights on, illuminating the entire studio that had several cutting tables, sewing machines and rails of shirts and waistcoats. Racks of ties were in the far corner. Mannequins wore the full ensembles of shirts, ties and waistcoats. Some items were pinned with other fabric samples, presumably to expand the colour range.

'I love these fabrics, Marck. The shirts are exquisite.'

He lifted two waistcoats down from a rail. 'I've backed these with a sea mist grey silk and a claret coloured satin–mix fabric. They work well but I told the buyers that my intention was to create a print for the back of the waistcoats. Now one of them is really interested in placing an order if they can see the finished designs.' He sighed heavily. 'I've been so busy getting the summer fashion show organised.'

'So you really are having a fashion show?'

'Of course. It's nothing too grand, just a showing in one of the hotels in the city to highlight the latest collections for the forthcoming season.'

'Do you think you'll involve the sewing bee?'

He ran his hand through his flurry of dark curls. 'I might have mentioned this to Craig this afternoon during filming but I...well...I wasn't really intending to do it.'

'That's a shame,' I said, though I wasn't particularly surprised. It had sounded like a throwaway comment made on the spur of the moment. Why would he want to include the sewing bee ladies in his posh event? I turned my attention back to the task in hand. Ideas were already starting to spring to mind. Marck's cufflinks made me consider a nautical theme. 'How about a ship's wheel and a yacht print?'

He nodded immediately. 'Yes, I like that, but the colours...'

I did a rough sketch on a bit of paper that was on one of the cutting tables. 'Imagine if the ship's wheel was a light burgundy shade, a mono print, on a deep burgundy background. It would create a subtle pattern. The sheen on the fabric would highlight the design. And we could do the same with the yacht.' I scribbled an outline of a yacht. 'Again, we'd use a lighter print on a darker background. It would look really classy.'

'Yes, yes...it would. Brilliant. Okay, if you could do a finished design for the ship's wheel and the yacht, I'll contact the printer. They can usually make up a fabric order within a day or two. Then I'll have the waistcoats finished with the new fabric to show the buyer.'

'I'll work on those tonight and you can pick them up in the morning. The designs are straightforward so I'll have them ready for you.'

'Thank you, Morag. I appreciate you going along with this.'

I went to leave but then he said. 'And if you think up any other designs...'

I nodded. 'I'll have a think and include another couple of ideas.' I didn't have them yet, but when I started to sketch designs I usually thought of other variations. Flowers were always one of my basic starting points but floral prints for menswear didn't quite work so easily.

Marck gave me samples of the wool fabrics that were used for the waistcoat fronts and a copy of the colour chart for his latest collection. Then he drove me back to the cottage.

'I'm sorry to put this pressure on you,' he said as I got out of the car, 'but I appreciate you doing this at such short notice.'

'I'll see what I can come up with.'

'We'll sort out the payment for your work,' he said, gazing at me with those intense blue–green eyes.

I nodded, trusting that Marck would indeed pay me the going rate, but as this was a rush job, there was no time to settle on the money issues. We'd deal with that later when the designs were ready for the printers.

I made a cup of tea and set to work, sketching the designs at the table in the living room. The cottage felt so quiet and calm and it was ideal for working late into the night.

I made more tea and eased the tension in my shoulders as I wandered back into the living room. That's when I noticed the fireplace. The evening had a chill to it and I attempted to light a fire using the method that Ruary had shown me. I brought several pieces of logs in from the pile behind the shed. It took a while to get going but once the wood started to burn a lovely warmth wafted from the fire. The logs crackled and sparked in the hearth as I continued to work on the designs. There was something comforting about having the fire lit on a night like this.

I finished the work, and ignoring that it was almost two in the morning, I made myself a couple of slices of hot buttered toast and a large mug of frothy hot chocolate. I settled down on the sofa in front of the fire to relax and enjoy it.

The designs lay finished, artwork ready, on the table beside my sewing machine. I'd drawn other designs along with the nautical patterns. I hoped Marck would like them.

I didn't intend falling asleep on the sofa. I woke up at eight in the morning. Sunlight streamed into the living room and the chirpy sounds of the birds in the garden made me realise I'd spent the night on the sofa.

I jumped up, showered and tidied myself up ready for Marck.

He arrived just after nine, eager to see what I'd come up with.

He studied my designs, nodding appreciatively. 'These are excellent.' Then he noticed the other designs I'd included.

'I know that floral prints aren't what you had in mind, but I thought that if I used certain flowers, it could work.'

'Some of these hardly look like flowers unless you look closely at the designs. These are very clever, Morag. I like them. What type of flower is this?'

I smiled at him.

He smiled back at me. 'What? Is it something special? Something I should recognise?'

'It's a zinnia flower. I thought it would be a nod to your aunt. And the flower isn't a common design.'

'Zinnia? This is great. I could use this as if it's part of the family tradition. And of course, my aunt will be pleased.'

'I'm glad you like it. I wasn't sure if you'd get what I was aiming for.'

'Oh I get it, Morag. I really do.'

'Can I offer you a tea or coffee?'

'No, I'm heading straight to the printers with your designs. They're friends of mine as well as business clients. They're going to try and print up a few metres of each design on to the silk fabrics today so that I can start making them up tonight.'

Before he left he took a cheque from his inside jacket pocket and handed it to me. He'd already written it with a generous amount of money.

'I trust this will cover your design costs?' he said.

I gazed at the figure on the cheque. 'It certainly will, Marck. But you hadn't even seen the finished designs.'

'I saw what you were capable of yesterday. Your portfolio of work is marvellous. I knew you'd come up with something suitable. I'll call you later and drop off some samples of the fabric.'

'Yes, I'd love to see how the prints come out.'

'See you later.'

I worked on my own designs during the day. I stopped for lunch and wandered out into the garden. It was a mild May day and the sun shone throughout the afternoon, finally casting an amber glow over the cottage by the early evening.

Marck phoned. 'The fabrics look fantastic. I'm working like blazes on the waistcoats right now. Can you drive over to the studio?'

'I'm on my way.'

I threw my jacket on, grabbed my bag and drove across the city. Even though I'd been designing for a while, I still got excited when my designs were printed on to fabric.

Marck welcomed me in. 'The kettle's boiled. Help yourself to a cuppa.' He hurried back to work on the waistcoats. He'd backed four different waistcoats with the new fabrics. He had people who worked for him, experts in tailoring, but he wanted to make these himself. They'd all gone home.

I brought my tea through and studied the fabric samples. 'These have come out great.'

'They've printed up a treat. The buyer will like them. I've got a good feeling about this collection.'

I watched him work, skilfully sewing the finishing pieces to the sample waistcoats. Jannet was right. Marck was an expert tailor and brilliant at sewing.

'What have you been up to today?' he asked, while concentrating on working away at the sewing machine.

'I worked on my collections. I got a lot done.'

'It feels good when you've had a productive day.'

'And night.'

He laughed. 'Yes, we've been working round the clock.'

'When I'm designing I just keep going. I don't care what time it is.'

'I'm like that too. I think it's part of the creative process, or we're simply just mad.' He finished the final seam and held up his handiwork. 'What do you think?'

'Perfect.'

'The buyer is going to be here at the crack of dawn tomorrow. I'll press these, hang them up and then we'll have dinner.'

'Dinner?'

'Unless you're dining with Ruary again this evening?'

'No, I'm not.'

'Fine. I should be finished within half an hour and then we'll get going.'

A thunderous sky cast a dramatic atmosphere over the city.

We went to one of Marck's favourite restaurants that had a panoramic view of the Glasgow skyline. We sat at a window table, high above the city, and drank a champagne toast to the success of the waistcoat designs.

I sipped my champagne and gazed out at the view. Hundreds of lights glittered in the stormy night and the River Clyde looked like liquid gold.

'Craig phoned me earlier this evening,' said Marck. 'We're going to be on the television tomorrow morning.'

'Did he say what time we're on?'

Marck told me the channel and time.

'I hope they include Jannet and the other women,' I said. 'They'll be so pleased if they're on the telly.'

'I phoned Jannet and she's going to tell the other women. Craig assures me that they are included, along with us, and Ruary.'

'Does Ruary know? Did you phone him?'

'No, I'll give him a call now if you like.'

I nodded.

Marck phoned him.

'Ruary, just to let you know that Craig from the television phoned. The sewing feature airs tomorrow morning. Tune in. It should be interesting.'

The conversation was short and not terribly sweet.

'What did Ruary say?'

'He was his usual casual self, although I bet he's keen to see himself on the telly. And he asked if you knew. I told him you did.'

'It's exciting, isn't it?'

Marck laughed and tucked into his meal. 'I suppose you thought you'd have a relaxing time when you moved into the cottage. Instead it's been manic, and now you're going to be seen by thousands of viewers.'

'I've had quieter times.'

'There's not much chance of those when you're involved with us. And I've been thinking about how to involve the sewing bee in my fashion show. I may have an idea.'

'Are you going to tell me what it is?'

'I'm not sure if you'll approve.'

'Sounds dubious.'

'It does, doesn't it?'

'Are you planning to ask the ladies to sew items for the show?'

'Something like that. I'd obviously have to discuss it with them, but I thought I'd run the idea past you first. My show highlights the new shirts, ties and waistcoats. I hire male models to wear the designs. That's basically it. Buyers turn up to view the collection as do other clients and customers. I thought I'd ask the ladies to design an evening dress, full–length or cocktail style, and include them in the show.'

'You want Jannet and the others to wear their handmade dresses?'

'Yes. What do you think? They'd have three weeks to sew their dresses.'

'I love the idea. I think the women could sew their own dresses. The only thing is...will they want to model them?'

'Jannet has a fine figure. Great legs. I think she could look quite lovely. And so could you.'

'Me?'

'Of course. You're part of the sewing bee now.'

Chapter Six

Cornwall, London & Paris

By the time we'd finished our pudding — a chocolate and cream confection, Marck had persuaded me to get involved in his fashion show. I blamed the deliciousness of the dessert coupled with Marck's charm that made me agree to sew and model an evening dress.

'It'll be fun and I'm sure the ladies will enjoy flirting with the male models, and vice versa.'

'You sound as if you're a matchmaker, Marck. Or should that be troublemaker?'

'A bit of both hopefully.' The twinkle in his blue–green eyes sent a thrill of excitement through me.

'I'd better start thinking about making a dress.' I'd no idea what to make. I didn't have many evening dresses.

'There's a theme to the fashion show — vintage, classic cocktail era.'

'I'll keep that in mind when I'm designing a dress. I've seen the colours you've used for the new waistcoats so I'll try to make it blend with those.'

'I have fabric swatches and colour charts in the car. I'll give you some so you can ask the ladies to sew a dress that would fit in with those. And if they agree to take part in the show, I'll contact Craig with the details. He told me to call him if the sewing bee ladies became involved. He wants it as a follow–up feature.'

Another flurry of excitement went through me, this time at the thought that we were going to be on the television the next morning.

'Are you okay?' he asked me. 'You've gone a bit pale.'

'I'm just thinking about being on the telly tomorrow.'

'At least I'll be able to watch it before I fly down to Cornwall on Saturday.'

'Are you going to visit your aunt Zinnia?'

'Yes, I'm organising things for the show and having a meeting in London. I'm flying down on Saturday morning. The meeting is in the afternoon. Then I'm popping down to Cornwall for a quick visit before dashing over to Paris and then flying back from Paris to Glasgow on Monday.'

'Sounds hectic.'

'It is.' He looked at me thoughtfully. 'Come with me.'

'To Cornwall?'

'Yes, come and meet Zinnia and my mother, Violet. She's got a shop in Cornwall, sewing related, but it serves up the most delicious cream teas. Sheer indulgence. I'm sure they'd love to meet you.' He explained that he'd lost his father years ago and that the shop had kept his mother going. She didn't want to leave it and move back up to Scotland, and that was why Zinnia travelled up and down several times during the year to visit her. 'It's like mid–summer down there already. The break would do you good. You look a bit pale and drawn — but still very, very lovely,' he added, leaning towards me across the table.

'Are you flirting with me? Jannet warned me about that.'

'Did she now?'

We smiled at each other and something in my heart melted when I gazed at him. He was flirting and I supposed he made a habit of it, though this didn't lessen the effect he had on me.

'So, will you come with me?'

'A whirlwind trip to London and Cornwall?'

'And Paris. I wouldn't leave you in Cornwall. I'd take you with me to Paris, then we'd fly back to Glasgow. You'd be home again by lunchtime on Monday, wondering why you ever agreed to such a crazy invitation.'

'Hmmm, that's not such a brilliant sales pitch,' I told him.

'It's the nearest to the truth. I think we both know that. Come on, what do you say? Say yes.'

I paused for a moment and then heard myself say, 'Yes.'

He poured us another glass of champagne. 'Here's to a wild time in Cornwall.'

We tipped the edges of our glasses together. I wouldn't normally have accepted his invitation, but since splitting with Gavyn, I felt that for the first time in two years I could do exactly what I wanted and that encouraged me to agree to go. Besides, a trip to London and Paris sounded exciting.

'I've never been to Paris or Cornwall,' I said. 'But I've been to London a few times.'

'I think you'll enjoy the tranquillity and the mayhem.'

I nodded. 'Cornwall always sounds wonderfully relaxing. Beautiful coastlines, rolling countryside and little towns and villages dotted across the landscape.'

'I was actually meaning the mayhem will be our trip to Cornwall. Although you're right about the beauty of it, there's no chance of a relaxing time when Zinnia and my mother are involved. You'll be cosseted, quizzed and well–fed. Once they know that you make sewing patterns...well...I may never be able to prise you away from them.'

I laughed. 'And I may never want to leave.'

'I think you'll love my mother's shop. Its haberdashery is addictive. Every time I'm there I want to buy the buttons, trims and silk fabrics. My mother adds new items to the stock every month. She trawls the internet for interesting products — the new threads are exquisite for hand sewing. I indulged and bought lots of colours from the range. So fair warning.'

'Warning noted. But it sounds like the type of shop I'd like to move into.'

'You never know...perhaps you will.'

We finished dinner and Marck drove me back to the cottage.

'Phone me tomorrow,' he said as I got out of the car. 'Let me know what you think after you've seen the telly feature.'

'I will do.'

He drove off.

I went inside and started to plan what I'd take with me to Cornwall and Paris. I couldn't settle, so I packed a suitcase to work off some of the nervous energy that was making me wonder if I was doing the right thing. I had work to do. I mentally argued with myself while filling my suitcase with a selection of separates that I could mix and match to create various outfits. I threw in a little black dress and a pair of heels. Anything else I needed I intended to buy when I was in London, Cornwall or Paris. I would indulge and splurge a bit. The thought of this made me even more unsettled so I made a cup of tea and wandered outside into the garden to breathe in the mellow evening.

I sipped my cuppa and felt myself unwind as the scent of the flowers and atmosphere of the cottage garden soothed my senses. Then I thought about Ruary and my senses went into overdrive. Was it really only the previous evening that I'd had dinner at his house? How quickly everything had changed. Now I was off on a whirlwind spree with Marck.

I took a gulp of night air and told myself to relax. I was answerable to no one now. I was single and could do what I wanted. And that's exactly what I intended doing.

Later I lay in bed thinking about Ruary's house and what it would be like to live there, to share the property. I loved his garden and the house, and it certainly solved the worry of where I'd go when the lease was finished on the cottage. And yet...

Marck's face flashed through my mind and I recalled some of the things he'd said earlier during dinner about meeting Zinnia and Violet in Cornwall. *'Once they know that you make sewing patterns...well...I may never be able to prise you away from them.'*

'And I may never want to leave.'

The morning flew in and I switched the television on just in time to catch the start of the feature. I settled down in front of the telly and hoped they hadn't done a hatchet job on us.

Thankfully, they hadn't, and it was great to see how they'd edited all the little pieces together to show us sewing, having tea and eating cake. Marck came across very well, as did Ruary. They both looked extremely handsome and I was sure they'd have a few women lusting over them.

A burst of excitement charged through me when I saw how lovely the cottage looked. I cringed when I saw myself, though I didn't look as pale as I'd thought I would. They'd included close-ups of me cutting out a paper pattern and then sewing a robin.

I listened as Craig explained about the increased popularity of sewing. While he spoke in a voice–over in parts, they cut to various shots of Jannet and the other ladies sewing.

I laughed when I saw Ruary trying to look as if he was adept with a sewing machine. It worked. I'd never have guessed that he couldn't sew and was just filling in because they needed some male eye candy.

My stomach tightened when I saw Ruary's muscled forearms and how blue his eyes were. Marck was a charmer for sure but there was something about him that made me accept his flirty nature. Likewise, Ruary came across as natural and straightforward.

They'd edited some of my comments to Craig which worked for the better and made me sound as if I really knew what I was talking about.

Overall, they'd presented the sewing as a friendly and popular activity. Other clips from different sewists from various parts of the city were included and I enjoyed watching what they were making.

My phone rang minutes after the feature finished. It was Jannet. I think she asked me what I thought of the show. It was difficult to decipher between the squeals of joy that were echoing down the phone at me.

'Yes, it was brilliant, Jannet.'

More squeals of delight from Jannet.

Hearing how hyper she was, and rightly so, I decided this wasn't the ideal time to tell her that Marck wanted our sewing bee to be part of his fashion show in three weeks time. No, I was worried she'd explode with excitement so I thought I'd tell her later.

'Ruary looked luscious, didn't he?' said Jannet.

'He did.'

'And Marck. I wouldn't be surprised if someone approaches them for other work. They're handsome–looking fellas.'

'Marck's invited me to go with him to Cornwall tomorrow. A flying visit. I'll be back on Monday before lunch.' I said it quickly and edited out anything else such as Paris and London. I wanted to gauge her reaction before I dropped those into the mix.

'You'll like Zinnia and Violet. They've got cheery natures.'

'Marck says Violet has a sewing shop that also serves cream teas.'

'She has. I've visited it. It's one of those quaint wee shops that's got everything you need for sewing. I wanted to buy lots of things.' She hesitated and then said, 'Did Marck just happen to invite you to go with him? Remember what I told you about him.'

'Yes, he has to go down to London on business so he's going to visit his mother and Zinnia while he's there. I did remember what you said. I know that he's using his charms on me, but I don't want to miss out on a great time in London and Paris either.'

Silence and then she said, 'London? And Paris?'

'Eh...yes, Marck has business meetings in both those cities. That's why he's flying down to London and then going to Paris via Cornwall. He says he tries to visit his mum and his aunt Zinnia when he's down in London. The trip to Paris is related to his fashion show three weeks from now.'

'Well, enjoy yourself, but watch you don't end up with a broken heart or a scandalous reputation because of Marck.'

It was good advice. She meant well.

'Thanks, Jannet.'

'What for?'

'For caring.'

'Well, you just mind your tail when you're gadding about with Marck.'

'I will.'

'And one more thing,' she added. 'Can you bring me back three metres of Violet's silky gold fabric. She'll know what one it is. It's a soft, shiny gold material, light as air but great for making a dress.'

'A dress? Has Marck phoned you?'

'About what?'

I told her about him wanting to involve the ladies in his fashion show. After more squeals of delight, she explained why she wanted the material.

'No, I just fancied making a dress. I could order the fabric from Violet, but I thought you could pick it up while you're down there. Now I suppose I'll be using it to make a vintage cocktail dress for the fashion show.'

'It sounds very glamorous.'

'I saw the pattern for the dress months ago and thought the gold fabric that Violet sells would be perfect. I fancy a bit of glam this summer.'

'I'll get the fabric for you. As I said, I'll be back on Monday so you can pick it up on Wednesday at the sewing bee or before that if you prefer. I'll phone you when I get back.'

'Thanks, Morag. Make sure you enjoy yourself, and I want to hear all the gossip when you come home to Glasgow. I've never been to Paris, so I'd love to hear what it's really like.'

'I've always wanted to go to Paris. When Marck mentioned it I almost said no, but then I thought — why not?'

'Exactly. I understand that you haven't known Marck long and going off with him on a wee fling could lead to heartache. But I've known him for years. Marck's okay. You'll come to no harm if you take his flirting for what it is. He's a natural charmer, and with his looks, he's used to women wilting over him. But I'm sure you can handle him.'

'He hasn't actually flirted that much with me. He asked me to design fabric patterns for the backs of his waistcoats, and we worked quite well together. I feel comfortable in his company, despite knowing he's got a twinkle in his eyes for the ladies. Maybe we'll just be friends.'

Jannet laughed down the phone. 'Yes, that'll be right. Friends with extras more like.'

The remainder of Friday was a frenzy of work. I settled down in the cottage and designed new patterns for the collections. Somehow this made me feel that it was fine to be flying off to London with Marck the next day.

I thought I'd hear from Ruary about us being on the television but there wasn't a peep from him.

I concentrated on my designs and tried not to take Jannet's advice too seriously regarding Marck, especially about being careful not to end up with a broken heart or a scandalous reputation. I had no intention of falling for Marck's charms, though a mild flirtation did have a certain appeal. After being duped by Gavyn it was nice to feel a little bit flirtatious. It wouldn't be anything else. He wasn't my type. The Marcks of this world belonged to gorgeous and glamorous women and that definitely wasn't me. No, we'd enjoy each other's company, and I'd meet Zinnia and Violet. I was looking forward to visiting Cornwall.

I added a few extras to my suitcase, sorting everything ready for the morning, and then went to bed at a decent time. I'd set my alarm for six. Marck sent a text saying he'd pick me up after breakfast and we'd catch an early flight down to London.

True to his word, Marck did everything he'd promised, and we chatted so much on the plane that the flight seemed to be over so quickly.

Marck hired a car at the airport and drove us down to Cornwall. His meeting in London was rescheduled for later in the summer and this gave us more time in Cornwall. The mild day in London soon brightened and became a scorcher as we drove down towards the Cornish coast. The wild but beautiful landscape stretched for miles along the rugged coastline and the sun glistened off the deep turquoise sea.

'Not far now.' Marck pointed towards a small town on the edge of the coast. 'See those white–painted cottages?'

'Yes.'

'The one next to the pale blue farmhouse–style building is my mother's cottage. She also owns the other property. It used to be a working farmhouse but it was converted years ago into a tea shop. We'll be staying above the shop. The cottage has two bedrooms. Zinnia is in the spare room so we'll have to share the flat.'

I gave Marck a look.

'Sharing the *two–bedroom* flat,' he clarified. 'Separate rooms. And you're on your honour not to put me into any compromising positions.'

I laughed. I liked the way he made me feel comfortable about things that I should feel the opposite about.

'I promise not to creep into your bedroom during the night,' I said.

'What about during the day though? I have my reputation to think of.'

We teased each other as he drove towards Violet's cottage and parked outside the tea shop.

A selection of fabrics were in one of the front windows of the shop along with sewing accessories. Two cake stands filled with a tempting array of fairy cakes and scones sat in the opposite window. Sewing fabrics and afternoon tea. The best of both worlds. Certainly my type of shop.

Two faces appeared at the shop window as we got out of the car. I saw that people were seated at the tables having afternoon tea and there were a couple of customers browsing the fabrics and haberdashery.

Marck smiled and waved at the two women. One had dark hair with soft curls and a statuesque build, while the other was blonde and petite. I assumed the former was Marck's mother, judging from the likeness, especially the dark hair.

Marck wrapped his arms around them and the three of them gave each other a hug. Then the woman with the blonde hair turned her blue eyes to me.

'You must be Morag,' she said, and gave me a hug that was as warm and welcoming as the one she'd given her nephew. 'I'm Zinnia, and this is my sister, Violet.'

Marck's mother stepped forward and I was given a second hug, and then we were ushered into the tea shop. Two staff tended the tables and were busy serving up tea, cakes and scones. The tea shop looked like it belonged to the past, the 1940s, maybe earlier. The vintage decor reminded me of Zinnia's cottage — the floral curtains, old–fashioned crockery, classic tables and chairs set with silver cutlery and cake stands on white linen table covers decorated with hand embroidery. The colours of the threads that created the petals of flowers and wings of butterflies had kept their vibrancy. Most other things had that lovely faded look of vintage quality.

Pictures of flowers were framed on the walls along with tea–themed wall quilts, and oak beams stretched the length of the tea shop with its rich cream walls and cherry–wine carpet.

The aroma of vanilla and home baking filled the air along with coffee and chocolate.

Marck's pale blue pinstripe shirt and herringbone waistcoat made him look like he belonged to the era. Although I wore a more modern ensemble of grey jeans and a fashionable print blouse, I felt that I was welcome there.

Chapter Seven

Fairy Cakes & Tea Quilts

'Would you like to have afternoon tea?' Violet said to me. 'Are you hungry? Or would you prefer to freshen up after your trip down from Glasgow?'

'I'd love a cup of tea.'

'And cake,' said Marck. 'You'll have to try the strawberry sponge with clotted cream, and the icing and buttercream on the fairy cakes is delicious.' He smiled at me. 'Resistance is futile.'

Without giving me a chance to resist, we were served afternoon tea with the tastiest cake I'd had in a long time. The melt–in–the–mouth icing on the fairy cakes blended perfectly with the buttercream filling. A caramel glazed cherry added the perfect touch.

'These taste amazing,' I said.

Violet smiled at me. 'Thank you. It's so nice to have you down here. When Marck said he was bringing you with him we were so excited, weren't we, Zinnia?'

Zinnia's blonde hair was pinned up in a bun and she had the clearest pale complexion. In some ways she reminded me of...well...me. How I'd look when I was older. Or perhaps she reminded me of my mum?

Zinnia nodded. 'Marck told me all about you when you moved into my cottage. I was so glad that you were a sewist. Having someone who appreciates sewing and making things felt reassuring. I thought you'd be the type of young lady who'd love the cottage and the sewing bee as I do.'

'I do love it,' I told her, while Violet slipped another fairy cake on to my plate. Resistance was totally futile.

And then I saw a look, a mischievous smile, between the two sisters.

'What about you and Marck?' said Violet. 'You seem to have clicked.'

I blushed as bright as the cherry on the fairy cake and hoped that Marck would take up the slack and explain that we were just friends.

Marck put his teacup down and looked thoughtful. 'I haven't proposed marriage yet —'

I almost choked on my cake.

Zinnia gave me a helpful pat on the back as Marck continued to wind me up by pretending there was a lot more going on than friendship.

Violet shook her head at him and then said to me, 'He's incorrigible, Morag. Always has been, always will be. We expect there will be a blue moon in the sky the day Marck decides to settle down and get married.'

Zinnia smiled and nodded in firm agreement. 'He's all charm and no substance. But we love him just the way he is.'

Marck faked a frown. 'I think I'm insulted.'

Zinnia laughed and ruffled his hair.

One of the waiting staff hurried over. 'We're getting really busy. The usual Saturday rush for more scones. And we need extra butterfly cakes.' His eyes were alight with mild panic. 'I haven't had a chance to stick the wings on to the buttercream.'

'We'll let you enjoy the rest of your tea,' Violet said to me and then disappeared into the kitchen along with Zinnia presumably to stick the wings on to the butterfly cakes.

While more customers arrived and every seat in the tea shop was taken, Marck told me more details about his mother and Zinnia.

'When we lost my father I was only a young boy but my mother never remarried. Zinnia's been married twice. She says she has no plans to marry again. She loves the cottage in Glasgow but during the past two or three years she's been thinking about moving down here to live with my mother.'

'What would happen to the cottage?'

'Zinnia wants it to stay in the family, so she would expect me to take it on, either live there myself or lease it out to someone like you.' He looked pensive. 'I have to say that I quite like the idea of living there myself. I was brought up between there and Cornwall.'

Marck's phone rang. 'Do you mind if I take this call? It could be about the fashion show or meetings in Paris.'

'No, I don't mind.' I'd automatically switched my phone off when we sat down to have tea. I hated taking calls while having something to eat, but under the circumstances I really didn't mind because this was a business trip.

'Hello,' Marck said to the caller. 'Yes, Morag's here with me.' There was a pause. 'No, you can't pop round tomorrow to the cottage. Morag won't be in.' Another pause. 'Because she's not in Glasgow. We're down in Cornwall actually.' He chatted briefly to the caller and then handed the phone to me. 'Ruary wants to speak to you. Something about chocolate daisies.' And then he whispered so Ruary couldn't hear. 'He sounds miffed that you're here with me. I think he fancies you and he's a little bit jealous. Nothing worse than a jealous man. Well, I take that back. A jealous woman is hellish worse.'

I took the phone off him before he could whisper any more nonsense. 'Hello, Ruary.'

'I tried to phone you but your mobile is switched off so I took a chance that you'd be with Marck. I was going to pop round to the cottage on Sunday with the chocolate daisies, but Marck's got you gadding about all over the country, so I guess I'll bring them on Wednesday. I assume you'll be back for the sewing bee.'

'Yes, we fly back to Glasgow on Monday from Paris,' I said.

There was the longest pause.

Marck raised his eyebrows and stared at me. The mention of Paris hadn't gone down well with Ruary if the silence was any indication.

'Marck said you were in Cornwall.'

'I am. We are. We're with Zinnia and Violet in Cornwall. However, Marck has business meetings in Paris on Monday.'

'And he's taking you with him to Paris?'

'He is. Is there a problem with that?' I didn't hide the annoyance in my voice.

'No, Morag. No problem. I'll see you when I see you.' And then he hung up.

Marck was eating a slice of cake and nodding. 'He's definitely jealous.'

'That's ridiculous. I barely know him. We had dinner but that was all. I haven't known you for long either but I feel comfortable being here with you.'

'Yes, but I'm different from Ruary. I'm frivolous. He takes things far too seriously. I once borrowed his cutting shears that he keeps in Zinnia's shed to clip my hedging. I didn't blunt the blades that much. Besides, that's what they're for, clipping and cutting. When he found out he accused me of ruining them. He can be overly dramatic.'

'Who can?' said Zinnia, coming back over to see that we had enough tea in the pot.

'Ruary. I was just explaining to Morag about the cutting shears fiasco.'

'Those were his specialist shears,' Zinnia explained. 'He's fussy about anyone using his equipment.'

'I replaced them, didn't I?'

Zinnia gave him a pursed–lipped look. 'With my pinking shears that I use for sewing.'

'That was a joke,' said Marck. 'I wanted to lighten things up.'

'Speaking of lightening things up, we'd like you to have dinner with us this evening, unless you've got a dinner date with Morag,' said Zinnia.

'What do you think?' he asked me, trying to sound serious. 'Is it okay if we cancel our hot date and wild night out this evening in favour of dinner at my mother's house?'

I played along. 'I suppose I could be persuaded.'

Marck smiled at Zinnia. 'She can, you know. I'm already a bad influence on her. She should be working hard on her new patterns but here she is in Cornwall with us eating fairy cakes and annoying Ruary.'

'Patterns?' she said to me.

'Yes, I design sewing patterns. I thought Marck would've mentioned this to you.'

'He said you loved sewing but I didn't know that you're a pattern designer.'

'Yes. I can't wait to have a look at all the materials you have in the shop. The colours and fabric range is wonderful.' From where I was sitting I could see the fabric part of the shop on the opposite side of the tea area. Shelves were stacked with rolls of fabric from silks to brocade, cottons to chiffon and everything else imaginable. Racks of sewing accessories were on display in the haberdashery corner and an old–fashioned dark wood counter encased the fabric area. 'Customers have been browsing since we came in and although I wanted to rush over and see everything I didn't want to interrupt a sale.'

'I'll show you the fabric later,' Zinnia promised. 'I think you'll appreciate the new ranges we've got for the summer.'

'Which reminds me,' said Marck. 'I brought samples of the fabrics that Morag helped design for my waistcoats. They're in the car. I'll show them to you later because there's something special in the designs that Morag added.' He winked at me. Obviously he hadn't told his aunt that I'd put zinnia flowers into the design. 'I've also brought a copy of the television feature that was on earlier today. I recorded it on to DVD. I thought we could watch it after dinner. You'll see Morag cutting a paper pattern and sewing a cock.'

'A robin,' I corrected him.

Zinnia laughed. She seemed like the type of woman who enjoyed a bit of light–hearted banter.

'You'll see the cottage on the television. It looks lovely,' Marck added.

Zinnia's blue eyes sparkled. 'Oh that would be wonderful. I can't wait to see it.'

We finished our afternoon tea and then Marck suggested we put our bags upstairs in the flat and then head out for a quick tour of the area before dinner. I had one small case while Marck had four suitcases and a carry–all.

He led the way upstairs to the flat, loaded with his suitcases. I helped him by carrying his bag.

'Suits take up an enormous amount of space,' he said in defence of his excessive luggage for the weekend trip.

'I assumed you had samples of your gents clothing in the extra cases.'

'Only my clothing. I brought three suits with me, waistcoats of course and several shirts. You can never have too many shirts or ties especially when you're trying to impress someone.'

'I understand. In your business you have to look presentable. Wearing your own menswear designs makes sense.'

He glanced over his shoulder at me. 'It's not my business clients that I'm trying to impress.' He nudged the door open at the top of the stairs and lugged the cases into the flat. We put our bags down in the living room that was decorated in the same vintage style as the shop. 'There's only one person I'm trying to impress this weekend — and that's you.'

'Me?'

He shrugged, picked up his cases and headed into one of the bedrooms. 'My thoughts entirely.'

I followed him. 'Why do you want to impress me?'

He put two cases on the floor and two on the patchwork quilted bedspread.

'I have no idea. I never bother trying to impress women. I've always relied on my charm and devastating good looks.'

'I don't know why a modest and unassuming man like you hasn't been snapped up.'

'I guess I'm just not marriage material.'

Violet knocked on the door. 'Can I come in?'

'Make yourself decent, Morag,' Marck called out to me.

Violet knew he was kidding and walked in carrying fresh groceries for us.

'I've brought you fresh milk and bread in case you want to make toast and a cuppa.' She put them through in the kitchen. 'Dinner will be ready at seven.'

'Great, I'll have time to give Morag a whirlwind tour of the town.'

Violet smiled at me. 'Don't let Marck tempt you into trouble.'

'What about me?' he said. 'What if Morag tries to tempt me?'

Violet shook her head at her son and then headed back downstairs to tend to the shop.

'Are you always like this?' I said to him.

'No, only when I've got an interest in someone who affects me in ways that are inconvenient. Under the circumstances, I'd prefer to spend time seeing my mother and my aunt and then concentrate on the trip to Paris. Instead I'm wondering if I've made a mistake inviting you to come to Cornwall with me.'

My heart sank. Part of me knew he was being flippant but his remark stung me nevertheless. 'I'm sorry if you feel like that.'

That was the moment he realised he'd overstepped the mark. 'I didn't mean to upset you.' He ran his hands through his thick dark hair. 'Listen, I admit that I could be attracted to you and because I actually like you I have no intention of taking things further.'

I looked at him and sensed he was telling the truth.

He continued, 'I'm sure Jannet warned you again about me. And she's right. My mother and Zinnia are right too. I have no intention of getting married and settling down. As I believe you do, when you meet the right man, which is obviously not that cheating rat, Gavyn,

I know one thing for sure — I'm definitely not marriage material and certainly not the man for you, Morag.'

I nodded and took in everything he told me. 'Luckily for you I have every intention of enjoying the trip to Cornwall, London and Paris without getting up to anything that I'd feel embarrassed about when I get back to Glasgow.'

'Great. I'm glad we've cleared the air. Now we can get on with the business of having fun.'

While he hung his suits up in the wardrobe, I put my case in the other bedroom. The decor was shades of soft lilac and pale lemon. I gazed out the window at the view of the sea dazzling in the hot, late afternoon sunshine. It looked more like the height of summer rather than May. I felt the heat of the sun shining through the window and warming the bedroom. I took my jacket off and stretched my arms wide, easing the tension in my shoulders that had build up without me realising.

The bedroom was small but I loved the quaint and cosy feeling of it. The sewist in me couldn't help but notice the skilfully stitched quilt on the bed. Lilac, lavender and amber colours in the pattern reminded me of spring, fresh and pretty.

Marck knocked on the bedroom door. 'Can I come in?'

'Yes, I was just admiring the view. The sea looks wonderful. It makes me wish that we were in Cornwall for a week and that I could go swimming and enjoy a break here. I haven't gone swimming in the sea since I was in my early teens.'

'Let's go now.' He sounded so enthusiastic.

'Eh...no, I was just voicing my thoughts. I haven't even brought a swimsuit with me.'

'You don't need one.'

'I'm not going skinny dipping, Marck.'

'I wasn't suggesting that for a moment, though the thought is very appealing. You've got a spare pair of jeans with you surely?'

'I brought one pair and I'm wearing them.'

'On second thoughts, you don't need them. You can wear one of my shirts over your undies. Very decent. The shirt will be big on you but it'll be fine.'

'You want me to go swimming in my knickers and your shirt?'

He was nodding at me. 'I brought my swimming trunks. Believe me, your outfit will be far less revealing.'

'Swimming trunks, huh?'

He nodded again.

'For the novelty value alone, I'll do it.'

He rubbed his hands together. 'Let's get going before common sense kicks in and you change your mind. Oh and…if my mother or Zinnia ask what we're up to lie or we'll never hear the end of it during dinner tonight.'

Agreeing that we'd head down to the shore, Marck threw towels, one of his shirts and other items that he seemed to think we'd need into a bag and we hurried downstairs.

'Off jaunting?' Violet said to us. 'Remember, dinner's at seven. But make sure you show Morag the shore. It's such a gorgeous day out there.'

'We'll drive down there right now,' he said and escorted me out to the car.

He put the windows down and we drove off with the warm breeze blowing into the car.

We reached the shore in minutes and Marck parked the car facing out towards the view. There were only a few people around and those that were left were packing up their deckchairs and windbreakers and driving back into the town as it was approaching teatime.

'Avert your eyes,' Marck told me.

'What?'

He reached over into the back seat and handed me a pinstripe linen shirt that I knew I'd have trouble giving back. I loved boyfriend shirts. Sometimes I searched vintage shops and markets for shirts like these. They were great for wearing around the house.

'I'm going to be bollock naked while I put my trunks on, so look out the window or put your shirt on. I promise not to peek.'

I slipped my top off and put the shirt on over my bra and knickers while Marck sounded as if he was wrestling to get into his skimpy trunks. I tried not to laugh, or to look.

'Oh bugger,' he said.

'What's wrong?'

'The elastic's knackered on these. I keep meaning to buy a new pair but I keep forgetting. I don't go swimming very often these days.'

I went to look at the elastic but he thought I was sneaking a look at him.

'You're peeking, Morag.'

'I'm not.'

'You are.'

'I was just trying to see if I could maybe tighten the elastic.' I rummaged in my handbag. 'I've always got spare safety pins with me.' I gave him one.

He accepted it eagerly and I glanced at where he was intending pinning it.

'Be careful where you stick it, Marck.' I tried not to laugh as he fiddled with the pin.

'There, that should hold them up long enough for me to make a total prick of myself.'

He took his shirt off and threw it on the back seat.

I kicked my shoes off.

'Are you ready?' he said.

'Yes.'

I expected Marck would look handsome and fit but I wasn't ready for the effect he had on me. When I saw him standing there in the sunlight in his sky blue, body–hugging trunks, I thought — wow!

He laughed at me. '*Wow?*'

Shit! I couldn't believe I'd said it out loud. Shit, shit. 'What I meant was — ouch. I stepped on a seashell.'

'You're rubbish at lying.' He smiled at me. 'So thank you for the compliment. It was a compliment, wasn't it? Wow sounds like a compliment to me.'

I blushed and ran away towards the water, feeling the warm sand beneath my feet. I spun around, letting the breeze blow through my shirt. 'I'm so glad I decided to come here.' The words were out without me trying to sound anything other than totally honest. At that moment, there on the shore, in the mellow sunlight with the water glistening for miles along the sandy coast, with Marck, it felt great. I couldn't stop smiling and I didn't want to.

Marck gave me a smile, a cheery wave, and then ran towards the sea. As with most men's swimming trunks, they left little to the imagination. This was a memory for the archives. I'd never tell him but he had the cutest backside and sexy as hell physique on him. But I think Marck knew that.

He dived into the water, and when he emerged, he smoothed his dark hair back from his face. The sleek look suited him. 'Come on, Morag.' He waved at me. 'The water's quite warm.'

Things were hotting up so fast that even if it had been freezing cold I'd still have been feeling the heat.

Wearing only my undies and his shirt I waded into the sea. The water felt wonderfully warm and fresh.

Marck lifted me up and I couldn't stop giggling. Then he threw me screaming into the sea. I swam under the water and broke through the surface behind him and splashed him without mercy.

We enjoyed a playful time in the sea that day. Friends, just friends, but with a lot more potential than either of us had intended.

Chapter Eight

Sewing Bee Dresses

'It's almost six–thirty,' I said to Marck. Where had the time gone?

We were still messing around on the shore, enjoying the sea and relaxing on a blanket on the sand.

'Mad dash back for dinner?' he said.

We nodded to each other, dried ourselves roughly with the towels he'd brought and then drove back to the flat.

The shop was closed but Marck had a key. We hurried upstairs and he let me have first dibs in the shower. There was only one bathroom so we had to share.

'I'll be quick,' I promised, grabbing my toiletry bag from my suitcase and dashing into the bathroom.

He glanced at me as if to say — yeah, right.

'I will. I'm fast,' I insisted.

'Women always take ages.' He sounded so sure of this.

'I have a technique,' I called to him as I cast my damp things off and jumped into the shower.

'What's your technique?' he shouted through to me as I turned the water on to full blast and swamped my hair with a couple of large dollops of shampoo to clear it of the sea water and sand.

'I don't fouter.'

'Sounds like a solid technique, Morag.'

We spoke to each other through the half open bathroom door. The shower curtain shielded my modesty.

'I can shower, including washing my hair, in less than seven minutes,' I told him.

'Seven minutes? How do you know? Do you time yourself? Is it some sort of female hobby that I've never been privy to?'

'No, I used to have one of those shower clocks and I couldn't help but try to outdo myself by beating the clock. I can shower in under five minutes if I don't have to wash my hair. And if I have to use conditioner that adds to the time. But I'm pretty fast.'

'I'm impressed. And I'm timing you. Two minutes down and counting. Better be quick.'

I put on a burst of speed.

'It sounds like you're trying to drown a duck in there. Are you okay or do you need assistance.'

'Nearly finished. Get ready to jump in.'

'You make it sound like a shower relay. Pass me the soap instead of a baton.'

I kept the shower running, jumped out and grabbed a large, fluffy white towel from the rail and draped it around myself. 'Don't peek, Marck.'

Marck was almost inside the bathroom by now. He had a white towel wrapped around his waist. It emphasised his leanly muscled torso. I tried not to look. I really did. But I couldn't help myself. How often does a woman get a treat like this?

We passed each other and our eyes met. Then he glanced in the mirror. Although it had started to steam up around the edges, my backside was in clear view to him. His lips curved into a wicked smile.

'You peeked,' I chided him.

'It was unintentional, I promise you.'

I heard him get into the shower and headed through to my bedroom.

'But you've got a very pretty bottom, Morag,' he called through to me. 'Not that I was peeking.' And then he laughed.

I smiled to myself, cast the towel aside knowing that he was in the shower and I was free to run around naked getting ready for dinner. I put on a floral print cotton dress that was easy to wear and looked nice for having dinner. I wore it with classic pumps and then set about drying my hair and applying enough makeup to make myself presentable.

I was sitting on the edge of the bed blow–drying my hair when Marck emerged from the bathroom.

'Eight minutes, Marck. I do believe I win.'

'First the bumblebee pincushion challenge and now the shower relay. Is everything with you a contest?'

'You bring out the competitive side of me,' I said teasingly. I flicked off the hairdryer and brushed my hair smooth.

'Whatever am I going to have to do to beat you?'

'I'm sure a man of your resources, wit and wiles will think of something.'

'When I put my mind to something, I usually do. So don't say you haven't been warned.'

'Duly noted.'

'Pretty dress by the way. Very fetching.'

I swished the hemline and gave him a cheeky twirl. 'I think it would suit someone taller. I've always wanted to be a tall, leggy blonde.'

'Whatever for? Where's the uniqueness in that?'

I blinked.

'You're quite lovely as you are, Morag. And besides, think of the advantages of being a petite blonde rather than a tall and leggy one.'

'I'm thinking, I'm thinking. Nope, nothing springs to mind.'

'Take that dress for instance. You'd need almost another metre to make it fit if you were taller. Think of all the dresses you'd need to buy extra fabric for. And then there's the toes peeping out the end of the bed on cold, wintry nights. For you, it's not a problem. I'm six–three and believe me I know what I'm talking about.'

'Being in bed with tall women on frosty nights?'

He gave me a warm–hearted grin. 'You are incorrigible.'

I shook my head. 'No, Violet says you're the incorrigible one, and mothers always know the truth.'

He laughed and hurried through to his room to get dressed, leaving me with a sense that we'd become a little bit closer.

We hurried to the cottage for dinner, having thrown the clothes we'd worn earlier in the washing machine so that his lovely shirt wouldn't get ruined by the sea water. We arrived just before seven to a warm welcome from Violet and Zinnia.

'Something smells delish,' said Marck. He'd worn a fabulous blue shirt and dark trousers. His silk–back waistcoat was one of his new designs. I recognised it from the ones that he'd shown me in his workshop. It emphasised his broad shoulders and lean waistline.

We went through to the living room. Violet's cottage was so pretty. There were elements that were similar to the cottage in Glasgow, but this one had more nooks, alcoves and oak beams. It was a real Cornish–style cottage with a large garden out the back filled with flowers, vegetables and a greenhouse. The back door was open letting the warm air drift in, and the scent of the roses mingled with the mouth–watering aroma of whatever was in the oven for dinner.

'Make yourself comfortable, Morag,' said Violet. 'We don't stand on ceremony here. I hope you like roast chicken and roast potatoes. And we've got fresh vegetables from the garden.'

'That sounds delicious. I hope you haven't gone to too much bother, though I do appreciate it.'

'No bother at all,' Violet assured me. 'We're so pleased to have the two of you here with us.'

Zinnia came scurrying through from the kitchen. 'The potatoes have crisped up a treat and dinner's ready to serve.'

They'd both worn summery cotton dresses and made an effort with their hair and makeup, so I was glad that I fitted in with them.

Marck and I sat down at the dinner table which was situated in a dining area between the living room and the kitchen. The table was set with blue linen and silver cutlery. A basket of home baked bread sat in the centre along with oatmeal rolls and a selection of condiments.

Marck got up and opened a bottle of white wine. He poured everyone a glass while Violet and Zinnia served up the roast chicken dinner. I opted to have gravy and all the trimmings. There was nothing to beat a home cooked meal and I'd worked up an appetite from all the frolicking at the shore.

'Did Marck show you round the town?' Violet asked me.

'He, eh...he did. It's a beautiful area of the country.'

'Morag went skinny dipping in the sea,' he said, cutting into one of the roast potatoes.

Violet and Zinnia brushed his remark aside, used to his frivolous comments. They didn't believe him and that made me want to laugh.

'Okay,' he relented, 'almost skinny dipping. She wore her undies and one of my shirts.'

Violet shook her head and smiled at me. 'He's such a rascal.'

'It's true,' he insisted.

I sipped my wine and gazed at him over the rim of my glass. Didn't I just look so innocent.

'Nonsense,' said Violet. 'Look at Morag. She doesn't look like she's been splashing around in the sea.'

'Yes, but —'

Zinnia interrupted him. 'Her hair is all shiny. I know what mine used to look like after I'd been swimming in the sea.'

'She's had a shower.' He glanced at me for backup. I remained mim and ate my dinner. 'She can shower and shampoo her hair in seven minutes. She's fast in the shower. Very fast.'

Violet and Zinnia exchanged a smile and then Zinnia said to me, 'Tell me about your pattern making.'

'Yes,' said Violet. 'We didn't know that you designed patterns and fabrics. I'd love to be able to do that but I'm just not artistic.'

We chatted about the design work, about the collections I was working on, and I promised to email them a few templates for quilt blocks and quilt patterns.

'I was admiring your tea quilts hanging up on the walls of the shop,' I said.

'We love sewing the tea quilts,' said Violet. 'Any time we see a pattern for a new teapot or teacup design we make it into a block and then end up constructing a tea quilt. You know how it is with sewing. Having a purpose to make something is part of the pleasure. I enjoy working with the fabrics and finding new designs and colour combinations.'

'I'll send you patterns I've made that you can use — teapots, teacups, fairy cakes and an afternoon tea design,' I said.

Having promised to email these to them, we chatted while eating vanilla ice cream with slices of peaches. It was so refreshing and the perfect pudding after the roast chicken.

After dinner Marck showed them the waistcoat fabric. He'd brought a couple of metres of the zinnia design printed on pink cotton silk.

Zinnia's eyes filled up when she saw the zinnia flower pattern on the material.

'Morag did this as a nod to you,' he told her.

She came over and gave me a hug. 'That's the loveliest thing anyone's done for me in a long time. Thank you, Morag.'

We all got a bit emotional and so Marck suggested we watch the DVD. He set it up and we settled down in the living room on the sofas to watch the television.

Zinnia asked him to show her the introduction again because it showed the cottage. He was happy to let her view it in detail.

Violet clapped when she saw her son on screen. 'There's Marck. Doesn't he look handsome. And there's Morag.' She gave my hand a squeeze. 'You look beautiful on the telly.'

Zinnia blinked and sat forward as if trying to see the screen better. 'Is that Ruary? What's he doing sitting at a sewing machine? He doesn't sew.'

Marck explained about the agreed set–up.

'Eye candy?' Zinnia smiled. 'Ruary's certainly a looker.'

'He hasn't a clue with that sewing machine,' said Violet, 'and yet...he gives the impression that he knows what he's doing.'

'That's what I thought,' I said. 'You'd never know that he was the gardener.'

'I'm surprised he went along with the whole idea,' said Zinnia. 'He's very straight down the line about things.'

'Morag used her womanly wiles to persuade him,' said Marck.

Violet's blue eyes widened. 'Did you, Morag?'

'No, of course not.'

'Ruary's got a crush on her,' Marck told them.

'That's not true,' I objected.

Violet and Zinnia looked at me hoping I'd elaborate.

'I had dinner one evening at his house, but...'

'He wants her to move into his house when the cottage lease is finished,' said Marck.

'To move into the part of the house he rents out,' I clarified. 'To pay a lease. It would certainly save me having to find another flat.'

'But he's jealous that she's down here with me in Cornwall and that we're going to Paris,' Marck added.

Zinnia looked at me. 'It sounds as if Ruary has a thing about you.'

'I only met him recently,' I said.

'My first husband said that he fell for me the moment we met,' said Zinnia. 'Love can happen slowly or Cupid's arrow can hit on target the first time you meet. They say you never forget your first true love, and even after all these years, I never have.'

The mood in the room dipped for a moment and then brightened again when Zinnia saw how great the cottage looked in the shots leading out into the garden. 'My curtains look fantastic,' she said. 'I'd been thinking of changing them but seeing them on the telly I don't think I'll bother.'

We watched the feature twice. Three times if you included rewinding to the bits that showed the cottage.

'Jannet's a talented sewist,' said Zinnia. 'We've been friends for years. I'm glad they showed her sewing skills. She's an expert seamstress. There are a few great sewists in our wee sewing bee.'

'Jannet asked me to buy her three metres of your gold fabric,' I told Violet. 'She said you'd know what it was.'

'The gold fabric, yes. I'll cut that for her tomorrow. What is she making?'

'A vintage cocktail dress for Marck's fashion show.'

'I've asked the ladies to be part of the show,' he explained.

'That's an exciting idea,' said Violet. 'Maybe the TV people will want to film that too.'

Marck nodded. 'It was Craig, the man you saw in the feature, who asked me if I was going to include them in my fashion show. I thought it was a great idea.'

'Are you taking part in it?' Zinnia asked me.

'Yes, but I haven't decided what type of dress to make.'

Violet was up like a shot. 'I know you'll probably design your own pattern but I've got plenty of glamorous vintage dress patterns in the shop.'

A door led from the cottage through to the shop. I followed Violet and Zinnia. While I flicked through the patterns Violet cut the gold fabric for Jannet.

'Don't skimp on it,' said Marck. 'Add another three metres for Jannet. I'm buying. It's the least I can do as she's now making it for the fashion show.' He sighed. 'Maybe we should choose fabrics for the other ladies. What do you think, Morag?'

'That would be very generous of you, Marck.' I gazed at the array of fabrics on the shelves. There were so many to choose from. I noticed that Violet had a shelve stacked with glitzy and glamorous fabrics that were ideal for evening wear. I went over and began to feel the textures and weights, trying to pick materials that were beautiful and yet easy to sew. Violet and Zinnia were happy to pull out all the fabrics from the glitzy collection, and together we chose silver materials, silks and satin in fuchsia pink, emerald, teal, blue organza and the same fabric in a deep cherry wine. Chiffon wasn't easy to hem but the colours were vibrant and so we included a selection of those.

'Buy whatever you think the sewing bee ladies will need,' Marck told me.

I saw a purple material that glittered under the lights. 'Denice loves purple. I think she'd like this.'

Zinnia cut four metres and added matching thread for each of the fabrics along with trims such as velvet ribbons.

I kept Marck's colour theme in mind when I picked the fabrics, hoping they'd blend with his menswear collection and yet give a burst of elegant colour to the dresses.

I scribbled everything down so that I could get an overall picture of what we'd chosen and what was missing to complete the materials.

'I think we've got everything we need,' I said, having thoroughly enjoyed browsing through the fabrics and the patterns.

'What about you, Morag?' said Violet. 'Is there anything you'd like for yourself? Even if it's not for the show, I'd like you to have something from me to remind you of your trip to Cornwall.'

I saw one fabric that I loved — a decadent turquoise silk that glittered like the sea we'd been swimming in.

Violet followed my gaze and pulled the roll of fabric from the shelf. 'This is one of my favourites. Would you like a few metres? It drapes like a dream.'

I let myself indulge, even though Marck insisted on paying for everything. Violet didn't want him to, but he wouldn't listen and paid for the pile of fabrics and vintage dress patterns we'd chosen. He asked her to send everything up to Glasgow by courier so that we didn't have to take them with us to Paris.

Violet reached up for a couple of patterns on display. 'I'll pop these in. The ladies can share them. It's a basic bolero that fits small, medium and large depending on which layout you use. They can trace what size they need.'

'A bolero always sets off an evening dress,' said Zinnia.

I agreed.

'And this is a pattern for an evening cloak.' Violet held up the other pattern. 'It's a vintage design and sews up a treat when made in velvet and lined with silk or satin. I always think that you need something special to wear with an evening dress. Putting on a coat or a jacket is fine, if you have a nice velvet jacket for instance. But how many times do you have a beautiful dress to go to a party or night out and then wear a standard coat with it? No, this is sheer luxury, and not difficult to make, especially for the sewing bee girls.'

I looked at the cloak pattern. 'Thank you, Violet. And you're right. I definitely want to try making a velvet cloak now.'

'Make it in midnight blue or burgundy. It'll go with everything. If you make one it'll be all you need. You'll have it for years,' said Violet.

I helped Violet and Zinnia fold up all the fabrics and put them into bags. What a stash we had for the girls back in Glasgow. There were going to be squeals of delight at the sewing bee on Wednesday.

Chapter Nine

Seaside Sewing

We went up to the flat just before midnight having had a great evening with Violet and Zinnia.

Our bedrooms were off the living room. I turned my bedside lamp on. It gave a cosy glow to the room. I'd left the door open, intending to have a glass of water from the kitchen before getting ready for bed.

Marck's room door was open too and cast enough light into the living room so that I didn't need to put the lamps on. I filled a glass with water and drank it in the kitchen before padding through in my bare feet to my bedroom.

Marck stood in the doorway of his room — a tall silhouette of masculine temptation. He'd taken his tie and waistcoat off and unbuttoned his shirt. It hung open, revealing the smooth, taut chest I'd admired when he'd been swimming. He looked so sexy standing there getting ready for bed.

'I wanted to thank you, Morag.' His voice sounded deep and genuine. No fooling around in his tone.

'What for? I'm the one who is having a great time here in Cornwall. It's the break I needed considering everything that's happened in the past month.'

'For taking a chance and coming with me.'

We exchanged a warm smile and my heart melted a little.

'Goodnight, Marck.' I headed into my room.

'See you in the morning.'

I lay in bed aware that he was in the next room. I wondered if he was sleeping. That was the last thing I remembered because I fell asleep and woke up refreshed, having had one of the most restful nights in a while. Sunlight streamed through the window. Another sunny day dawned bright and clear.

I got up and gazed out at the view of the sea and the cloudless cobalt sky that stretched for miles along the coast. I could understand why Violet wanted to live here and why Zinnia might decide to leave her cottage in Glasgow. I wasn't sure what I would do. Probably travel up and down from Glasgow to Cornwall and enjoy both worlds.

Marck knocked on my door. 'Are you decent?'

I grabbed a sheet from the bed. 'Yes.'

A tray rattled and he carried in our morning tea.

'I thought we'd have a cuppa before going to the cottage for breakfast. My mother and Zinnia will have gone over the score baking fresh bread and rolls for us. They always have Sundays off to sew and relax. The shop is closed today. But when I'm here they make a full breakfast and it's definitely worth getting dressed for.'

I accepted the cup of tea and took a few sips. 'I'll jump in the shower and be right with you.'

He'd showered, shaved and wore coffee–coloured linen trousers and a shirt that was five shades lighter. Very classy. His hair was still damp and the unruly dark curls had yet to fight their way back up from the smooth style he'd given himself. In the morning sunlight he looked particularly handsome and my heart gave a little squeeze of acknowledgment that he was here with me, bringing me tea.

He cupped his tea and headed out of my bedroom. 'See you in four minutes.'

'Four minutes?' I followed him out.

'You surely won't need to wash your hair. It looks lovely and you only washed it last night,' he reasoned. 'By my calculations that would take another two minutes off your shower time.' He smiled at me over his shoulder and went into his room.

I knew he was joking but I hurried up anyway in case he was timing me. I was in and out of that shower in record time.

Back in my room I threw on another cotton dress. A vintage floral. The day looked as if it was going to be a scorcher and this was one I'd made myself from a tea dress design fabric. It was cool and comfortable to wear and bridged the gap between casual and tidy. I wore it with comfy pumps, brushed my hair and pinned the sides back with butterfly clasps. A brush of mascara and sweep of lipstick and I was ready to rumble.

We all had breakfast together in Violet's cottage. The smell of fresh baked morning rolls filled the kitchen. We sat around the kitchen table. I had orange juice and a soufflé omelette and one of the rolls. I also drank copious amounts of breakfast tea.

Marck was going to see a local tailor on business, so I decided to spend a sewing day with Violet and Zinnia. Marck did invite me to go with him, but he emphasised that I'd have more fun with his mum and his aunt. I opted for that.

After Marck left we set about planning our sewing day.

'Is there anything in particular you'd like to sew?' Violet asked me. 'I'm working on a quilt so you're welcome to work on some of the blocks with me. Zinnia's making us tops from a soft, stretchy fabric that's ideal for T–shirts and summer tops. With the weather getting warmer we thought these would be handy. We make a lot of our own clothes. Not all of them, but things like tops, blouses, dresses and skirts. Every time we get a new fabric in we're always tempted to make something with it.' She held up a primrose yellow material and an aqua and white patterned fabric. 'It stretches well so you don't need to fuss with zips or buttons. We both use the same pattern and adjust the size. Zinnia's a small size and I take a medium.'

'I love the look of the top,' I said. 'I make my own tops and blouses but this design has a pretty neckline and I like the option to shape the cap sleeves in various styles.'

'Right,' said Violet. 'Let's go through to the shop and choose a fabric.'

'This fabric here is easy to sew.' Zinnia pointed out the stretchy jersey–type fabric that she was using for her top. It was available in spring and summer colours ranging from lilac and lemon to aquamarine and pink. They also had basic neutrals but I liked the lilac. It reminded me of the bedroom decor and I'd taken quite a fancy to it.

I ran my hand along the bale of lilac material. 'I like this. I don't have anything in lilac.'

'I'll cut a metre of that for you,' said Violet. 'Nice choice.'

'Yes,' said Zinnia. 'It's a pretty and fresh colour. It'll suit your colouring.'

We went back through to start sewing, but not before a pot of tea had been made.

A cutting table was set up in a corner of the lounge. I traced a copy of the pattern which comprised of only a few pieces, and then began pinning it together ready for sewing.

Zinnia filled a bobbin with lilac thread and set up the sewing machine for me.

'There you go,' she said. 'I noticed in the television programme that you were very handy with a sewing machine so you'll have no bother using this.'

I sat down at the machine and began stitching the seams. The machine whirred cheerfully along the fabric and for a moment I realised how content I was. The sun shone through the windows, and we enjoyed our tea and sewing in the lounge with a view of the garden. The scent of sweet peas and roses wafted in, reminding me of the flowers in the cottage up in Scotland.

We chatted and I told them about Ruary and the chocolate daisies.

Violet was busy quilt making, edging a little cottage quilt with blanket binding ribbon.

'Ruary is a handsome young man,' said Zinnia. 'A decent sort, loves his vintage gardening. You could do worse than get involved with him. If I was younger, well...'

Violet sighed and continued stitching. 'It's a shame our Marck isn't the type to settle down. The two of you make a lovely couple and you seem able to sort him out. I don't like to undermine any woman, but some of the girls he's dated in the past have been far too hoity–toity. He's dated a few. Beautiful girls but always fussing with their hair, makeup and clothes. I can't picture any of them going semi–skinny dipping in the sea.'

I glanced round at her.

She shrugged. 'Gossip travels fast in a wee town like this. We got a tip–off this morning from a gossipmonger who saw the two of you.'

'There is always someone who sees you,' said Zinnia. 'Not that we think what you did was silly. At your age we'd do the same.'

Violet got out the cutting mat, rotary cutters and scissors and started piecing together another little tea quilt while chatting about everything from men and romance to sewing, knitting, embroidery and baking.

Violet was a keen baker and baked fresh bread most days for the tea shop. She kneaded the dough for two loaves and then let them rise for a couple of hours while we sewed. Then she kneaded them again and allowed further rising before popping them into the oven.

'Fresh bread for dinner,' she said, then realised that perhaps we had other plans. 'We don't want to take up your time with Marck.'

'I'm happy to sew with you and have dinner all together again tonight. Marck and I have Paris and then we'll both be back in Glasgow. This is like a wee holiday for me.'

We stopped sewing to have a light lunch. I'd already sewn my top together and tried it on for a fitting. Zinnia helped to adjust the shoulder line and made sure the hem was straight. Apart from that it was finished and ready to wear.

'That was a really easy top to make,' I said. 'Can I take this copy of the pattern with me. I'd definitely use it again, and Jannet and the others would make use of it too.'

'Certainly,' said Zinnia.

My sewing day with the girls was one of the most relaxing and rewarding in a long time. By the late afternoon we'd sewn ourselves silly, eaten cake and scones and drank lots of tea. I wasn't sure I'd have room to eat dinner, but then the savoury aroma reset my appetite and as we didn't actually sit down to the meal until after seven in the evening, I was ready to enjoy it when Violet and Zinnia served it up.

Marck had been busy at the tailoring shop and then whizzed around to another two business friends while he was out. He was back around six and keen to see what we'd been up to. He loved my top and I sensed that he was happy that we'd had an enjoyable day together.

After a relaxing evening at the cottage, I strolled along the shore with Marck. A gleaming sunset lit up the coast and turned the sea to liquid gold. I breathed in the warm air and walked beside him, chatting about everything. Marck was easy company, probably the first man I'd felt so comfortable with. Then we went back to the flat.

We got ready for bed, sharing the bathroom, crossing paths via the living room and kitchen. I tried not to think that this was the last night we'd be here. I didn't want to feel sad.

In the glow of the living room Marck paused and looked at me. Again, he wore his shirt open, unbuttoned. From habit or was he trying to seduce me? I wasn't sure and I don't think he was either.

He smiled at me. 'I'm tempted to give you a goodnight kiss, but I'm concerned where it could lead. I don't want to make any promises that I know I'm not able to keep.'

'One kiss wouldn't do any harm, would it?' I was aching for him to kiss me. Just once, to make the day complete, to see what those sensual lips of his felt like against mine.

He leaned down, pulled me close and kissed me deep and passionate, sweet but sexy. Finally, he let me go. We both understood we couldn't take things further. Not tonight. Perhaps not ever.

In hindsight, I shouldn't have asked him for that one kiss. I should've smiled and agreed that a kiss was not a good idea and gone to bed never knowing how great a kisser Marck was. I don't know what he thought, but the look in his eyes had a melancholy quality mixed with deep passion.

I think we both knew that we wanted and needed different things from life. I loved my work and had no intention of giving it up, but I also wanted to settle down and get married. Being a little bit wild was fine, but the truth was that Marck was a beautiful distraction, a man who was a summer fling, and after what had happened with Gavyn the last thing I needed was another relationship that was never going to go the distance.

'Goodnight, Morag.'

I nodded and went to bed.

We had a very early start. Up at the crack of dawn, said our goodbyes to Violet and Zinnia, although they planned to come up to Glasgow for Marck's fashion show and we'd see them again soon. Then it was a drive back up to London, drop off the hire car at the airport and catch the first available flight to Paris. Whirlwind to say the least. But we managed to do all of that, helping each other. We were, I decided, better off as friends, without the pressure of a fleeting romance and the inevitable heartache.

I gazed out the window of the plane as we flew over Paris. The excitement of the city rose up to meet me and I couldn't wait to see what it was like.

'They say it's one of the most romantic cities in the world,' Marck said as we took a taxi to a hotel he used whenever he was there on business which was two or three times a year.

'Is that a subtle hint?'

'No, it's a ruddy billboard of a hint. Last night...well...I was tempted to take things further. But it's better that we don't, isn't it?'

He sounded as if he needed my assurance. 'Definitely.'

He smiled at me, relaxed back in the taxi and took in the view of the busy Monday traffic. Dressed in one of his immaculate suits, he looked every inch the menswear fashion designer.

'The first meeting is in the hotel. We'll have lunch in the hotel restaurant. Come with me to meet a couple of the buyers that are also friends of mine. You'll like them. They're like me.'

'Trouble?'

He laughed. 'Absolutely, though I think you've got us all trounced when it comes to causing trouble.'

Chapter Ten

The Cocktail Dress Fabrics

Marck booked us into the hotel — adjoining rooms. Everything was on a tight schedule so we barely had time to relax before we had to get ready for the lunch meeting in the restaurant downstairs.

I wore a white silk blouse and grey linen trousers. The restaurant was upmarket and stylish.

Marck introduced me to his friends, both in the gents tailoring and fashion business. We dined on the finest French cuisine while discussing new ranges of clothing. By the time the meal was finished, the buyers had agreed to distribute items from Marck's new waistcoat collection in various outlets. A further meeting was scheduled for later in the summer in London.

It was interesting to see how Marck conducted his business and to see another side of the industry that I was part of. But I found my thoughts drifting, thinking about the sewing bee in Glasgow and how I wished I'd been able to stay longer in Cornwall.

We went back up to our rooms when the lunch meeting was finished. It was done and dusted in just over an hour.

'The next meeting is later this afternoon,' said Marck, standing gazing out the window at the city. Paris looked exquisite in the sunlight with its amazing architecture stretching out as far as we could see. 'Would you like to go sightseeing? We'll have the evening free to catch a show and have dinner, but if you'd like to put on a pair of comfy shoes rather than those heels, which are really chic, we'll go exploring the streets of Paris before the meeting.'

I went through to my room, kicked off my heels and slipped on a pair of flats.

We headed out and as we walked down a cobbled street and then further on into one of the famous boulevards, I breathed in the atmosphere of a city that seemed so familiar because I'd seen it in films, read about it in magazines, and now I was walking through it with this handsome man beside me.

I saw the Eiffel Tower but we didn't go up it. There wasn't time. Marck wanted to show me some of the fabulous designer shops and I succumbed to the lure of the window displays which were like works of art.

We stopped at a boulangerie that sold numerous types of bread and pastries. Marck bought us chocolate filled pastries that melted in the mouth. Then we headed to the second meeting in a vintage cafe where the buyer greeted us warmly and insisted we have our coffee and tea sitting at a table outside watching the world go by. The meeting ended on a similar note to the first with a further meeting set up in London at a fashion event.

An amber glow draped itself over the city as the daytime ended and the evening began. The air was warm and we decided not to go back to the hotel but to take in a show. We tried a couple of venues before finding one that had tickets available. We sat entranced and entertained by the whole spectacle of music and dancing.

'Are you enjoying yourself?' Marck asked me.

'Yes, it's amazing and everything I thought it would be. This is a city I'd love to spend more time in.'

'We'll come back one day.'

I smiled and didn't want to hold him to such a promise.

It was almost ten at night by the time the show finished and we wandered through the streets admiring the shop windows with their magnificent displays.

'If you see anything you like, let me know and I'll buy it for you,' he said.

I shook my head.

'You have to have a memento of your time in Paris,' he insisted.

'I don't need anything. I'll never forget this day. Never.'

Despite what I'd said, I let him buy me one thing — a silver thimble, to take back with me to Scotland. I saw it in the window of a silversmith shop and when he saw it catch my interest he went in and bought it for me. The shop was open late.

'Thank you, Marck. It's beautiful. I'll treasure it and I'll use it for sewing.'

He gazed down at me and smiled. 'Don't forget about...everything...when we get home to Glasgow.'

I held the little velvet gift box with the thimble inside it. I clasped it in my hand. 'I won't forget.'

He smiled and we walked back to the hotel.

Another night was almost over.

He knocked on the adjoining door. 'Can I come in?'

'Yes.' I was just getting ready for bed.

'We're up early again tomorrow. I've booked our flight.'

'I'll make sure I have everything packed and ready to grab and run,' I said.

He nodded and turned to leave. Then he glanced back. I thought he was going to say something, and I think he was, but changed his mind and just smiled at me instead.

I climbed into bed and gazed out at the view. I fell asleep admiring the lights of Paris glittering under the clear night sky. What a beautiful city, and a beautiful night.

'We're hellish late,' Marck shouted, dashing into my room the next morning.

Thankfully, I was already showered, dressed and ready to go.

We made our flight with minutes to spare.

During the flight we agreed that we both had a full working day ahead of us and a busy week, but we'd keep in touch and he'd come to the sewing bee on Wednesday to chat to the ladies about the fashion show. The fabrics from Cornwall were due to arrive on Tuesday by courier.

'Can I tell Jannet you bought the gold fabric for her?'

'Yes, and you can tell her about the other fabrics. Tell her whatever you want.'

'Great. I promised her I'd phone when I got back to Glasgow and I'd like to tell her what happened in Cornwall.'

'Minus the kissing?'

'That's just between us.'

'Jannet has ways to inveigle gossip out of people.'

'I'll dazzle her with thoughts of glistening fabric and vintage dress patterns.'

'Sounds like a plan.'

The cottage felt calm and welcoming when I arrived back. Marck dropped me off but didn't come in. He dashed off to his get on with his busy day.

I unpacked my suitcase, popped out to the local shop for fresh milk, bread and other groceries, and settled back into my own routine.

I opened the patio doors and let the air blow gently into the living room. It was another mild, sunny day. I made tea, put the silver thimble in my sewing basket and set up my table to start working on my designs. I planned to call Jannet when the phone rang.

It was Jannet. 'All hell's broken loose.'

Her words jarred me.

'Since you've been gone, people have been phoning up about the sewing bee, wanting to know if they can learn to sew, asking about fabrics and patterns. We've had lots of people stopping Denice, Sharla and me in the street. We're sort of famous now that we've been on the television. The interest in our wee bee has gone through the roof.' She spoke as if she was well wound up.

Her mild panic transferred itself to me. 'There won't be room at the cottage for lots of people.'

'I know, I know that. So we've been having emergency meetings. Sharla's ex–boyfriend, one that she's still talking to, works at a hotel that has a function room for hire. We were thinking of hiring it on a Monday night for all the people that want to come to the sewing bee.'

'So we'll have two sewing bees?'

'Yes, the Monday night is for everyone. Wednesday afternoons are just for us. At least until all the furore calms down. Some people might lose interest, others will turn up and join in. We won't know how many new sewists will be part of this. We're going to charge a small fee to cover the cost of hiring the function room. That seems fair, doesn't it?'

'Yes, it does.'

'I was going to phone you in Cornwall but we decided to try and handle the situation and let you enjoy yourself with Marck. How did things go? Did you...you know...?'

'We had a wonderful time and I really like Violet and Zinnia.'

'They're lovely, aren't they? But what about you and Marck? Did he kiss you? Was there snogging in Cornwall or Paris?'

'No snogging in Paris.'

'Oh, so there was kissing in Cornwall, eh?'

'I didn't say that.'

'Don't worry. I won't tell anyone except the girls. We'll keep it to ourselves.'

I told her about the fabric. 'I got your gold fabric. It's got a few extra metres in it.'

'I'll settle up the money with you on Wednesday.'

'Marck paid for it.'

'Really?'

'Yes and he's bought a whole load of fabrics for the other ladies. I chose a purple fabric for Denice and there are plenty of dress fabrics for everyone. Marck paid for them, and there are patterns included and trims such as velvet ribbon. They're being delivered to the cottage on Tuesday. Marck's coming to the sewing bee on Wednesday to discuss the fashion show.'

'Oh, I can't wait. I'll tell the others. Thanks for everything you've done, Morag. But there is one thing you should know.'

My heart sank.

'Women have been asking about Marck and Ruary. Lusting over them. I've been inundated with calls and even that man, Craig, from the television came round to my house because he couldn't get an answer at the cottage to see if Ruary was available to chat.'

'Chat about what?'

'About women lusting after him I suppose. And Marck.' She paused. 'Should we warn Marck that he's catnip to women at the moment?'

'Eh, no...he's busy. Besides, he'll find that out for himself, won't he?'

'Yes, I think Marck can handle the situation. But Ruary isn't happy. He's phoned me three times to complain and asked me to teach him how to sew. I told him to come along on Wednesday and we'll teach him the basics.'

'Ruary wants to learn to sew?'

'Not really, but he has to now because everyone thinks he can sew after seeing him on television.'

'It'll all fizzle out soon I'm sure.'

'Yes, we just have to ride this fiasco out. And how difficult will it be to teach Ruary to make a quilt or a shirt?'

'Exactly.' Which reminded me about the shirt I'd purloined from Marck. I'd squirreled it away in my case with no intention of giving it back to him. The fabric felt so soft and smooth against my skin and I loved the pinstripe colours.

'Are you still there, Morag?'

'Yes.' *Just thinking furtive thoughts.*

'Keep in touch. I'll see you on Wednesday.'

'I'll phone to confirm that the fabrics have arrived. They should be here tomorrow.'

I'd just finished the call with Jannet when Ruary phoned. He sounded dour. 'I assume you know what's happened.'

'Yes, all hell's broken loose, according to Jannet.'

'That about sums it up. So can you teach me to sew?'

'Of course. You'll pick it up in jig time.'

'I'll come round on Wednesday.'

It was going to be a full house for the next sewing bee. Glitzy fabrics, lots of women draping material around themselves and fighting over the fabrics. A grumpy gardener. And Marck misbehaving.

I scheduled mayhem and mischief on Wednesday, and then concentrated on getting some work done.

The fabrics arrived on Tuesday.

I phoned Jannet, listened to her squealing with glee for several minutes, promised I'd bake fairy cakes and scones for the sewing bee and said I'd see her on Wednesday.

I managed to finish a few of my designs and patterns on Tuesday. The day was mellow and I used it to recharge my emotional batteries knowing that every ounce of energy would be zapped out of me by the time the Wednesday sewing bee was over. Although it was scheduled for 2:30 p.m. until 4:30 p.m., I sensed that some of the women would arrive early to get first dibs on the dress fabrics, and with everything that had to be done, it was probably going to run until around 6:00 p.m.

The sun shone through the kitchen window on Wednesday.

I iced the fairy cakes. Having enjoyed the caramelised cherries on the cakes down in the tea shop in Cornwall, I dipped the cherries in caramel to create the same effect. Or as near to it as I could manage. I drizzled icing on the lemon drizzle cake, and took a batch of scones out of the oven.

It was barely 1:00 p.m. I was so busy I didn't bother having lunch and kept going. It was the right decision because several women, including Jannet, Denice and Sharla, turned up at the cottage eager to see the dress fabrics.

I'd folded them and put them on the dining table in the living room so that everyone could get a fair look at them. Jannet's gold material shone like a sunbeam.

The women gasped when they saw the array of gorgeous stash.

'Obviously the gold fabric belongs to you Jannet,' I said. Her face lit up from the glow of it and she couldn't thank me enough.

While Jannet stood entranced, the other women circled the table eyeing the fabrics, accessories and vintage patterns.

'The purple material is the one I picked for you, Denice, but you don't have to take it if you don't want to.'

Denice lifted the fabric up. 'I love it. Purple is my favourite colour and this is going to make a glamorous dress.'

Sharla had her eye on the pink organza. 'This is fabby. You know that I love pink.'

'Organza isn't easy to work with,' I said, making sure she understood what she was letting herself in for. 'The hems could be finicky.'

'I'll show you how to make a rolled hem. The old–fashioned way,' Jannet said to her. 'You can use your machine, but you'll get a lovely edging if you hand sew them.'

Sharla looked at me.

'Take the pink organza.' I gave her an encouraging nod.

Sharla held it up to the light. 'It's so sheer. I'll need a silk base.'

We chose one of the pink silks in a deeper shade of pink than the organza. So that was Sharla sorted.

Other women arrived and went wild over the fabrics and about the news that they were part of Marck's fashion show.

'You've got three weeks to finish the dresses in time for the fashion show,' I told them. 'And there will be a dress rehearsal.'

They agreed to help each other and seemed up to the challenge.

I explained about the extra patterns. 'Violet added two special vintage patterns — one for a bolero that can be altered to fit different sizes, and the other is to make a cloak. She suggests that anyone who makes a cloak uses velvet and lines it with silk. The colours that work well she says are midnight blue and burgundy.'

Jannet picked up the cloak pattern. 'How romantic. I quite fancy making one.'

'So do I,' I told her. 'I've read over the pattern and although we'd need quite a few metres of velvet, the actual construction doesn't seem too difficult.'

Jannet studied the picture on the front of the pattern. 'I love working with velvet. I know a shop where we can buy velvet wholesale if a few of us want to share the material.'

Denice peered at the pattern. 'I wonder if I could make a shorter version, like a cape, not a full–length cloak?'

Jannet flipped the pattern over and read the back of it. 'Yes, you could make that easy enough. They've even got a cutting line for a cape length.'

Denice nodded. 'Okay, I'm in on the velvet.'

I left them to decide what fabrics they'd like and went through to the kitchen to boil the kettle for tea.

Although I'd anticipated mayhem and mischief, there wasn't a hint of it until Marck and Ruary turned up at 2:30 p.m. By the time they arrived most of the ladies had picked the fabrics they wanted for their dresses and there were plenty of pieces of fabric to spare. Most of them were making cocktail dresses. Evening bags and purses were already being planned.

Ruary arrived via the front door. No climbing over the garden wall. Marck and Ruary parked their cars within minutes of each other outside the cottage.

Ruary had a gardening tray of chocolate daisies with him ready for planting.

They acknowledged each other with a rival's nod.

Marck glared at the chocolate daisies. He'd arrived empty–handed and his expression showed that he wished he'd brought something with him, preferably flowers.

I let them in. Two handsome men amid the ladies sewing bee. I sensed we were going to have a lively afternoon.

Chapter Eleven

Pincushions & Quilts

Ruary was dressed in jeans but he'd worn a shirt that wouldn't have looked out of place on the rails beside Marck's designer shirts. The pale vanilla pinstripe suited his blond colouring. His hair was the tidiest I'd seen it and I sensed he'd made an effort to look smart. The effort wasn't wasted because the women admired him when he walked into the living room.

He headed out to the garden and put the chocolate daisies in the shed. 'I'll plant these for you later,' he called to me, and then came back in.

'I hear the press are interested in us,' Marck said to him.

Ruary nodded curtly.

'Handsome men who can sew?' said Jannet. 'Of course they're interested. Craig told me there have been lots of calls and emails about the sewing feature — especially about the two of you. Sewing and sex appeal. I think that's one of the angles Craig mentioned to me for the follow–up feature. It'll include your fashion show, Marck. So that will be great publicity for you.'

'It will,' Marck agreed, 'and I'm pleased that the ladies are going to be involved in the show.'

The women thanked Marck for buying all the fabrics and accessories for them. He smiled happily and didn't make a fuss of this, deciding instead to focus on them and what type of dresses they planned to make.

And all the while Ruary sat there looking angrier by the second. His blue eyes darkened to a stormy blue–grey and I was waiting for him to let rip with whatever was bothering him.

Marck advised the ladies how to create the perfect edge on a silk garment, and that was the tipping point. As Marck explained his technique and then sat down at one of the sewing machines, using a remnant of silk from my fabric stash to show them how to give a professional tailoring edge to a seam, Ruary finally spoke up.

'It's okay for all of you,' he said, sounding huffy. 'You can sew. I'm the one who is the fake. The press are interested in chatting to me. I've already had them on the phone, and I think they suspect that

I'm a fake. Local magazines want to do features and see the things I sew. They can see what Marck makes — the shirts and waistcoats he designs and sews. It's all part of his business and on his website. But my business is vintage gardening. That's what's on my website. There's nothing about sewing and I think they're sharp enough to suss out that I was only put in to make up the male numbers in the sewing bee. If the press find out that I can't sew and put the story in the newspapers that I was on the telly pretending to be something I'm not, it could adversely affect my business. I need to be able to sew. And I need to learn fast.'

Every teacup had settled in its saucer. No tea was slurped. No cake nibbled or scone consumed.

We realised that he was correct. Ruary's reputation was on the chopping board. The press could cause ructions for him if they found out. Craig would be implicated. There would be nothing but trouble.

'I'll teach you to sew,' I promised him. 'Drop by every day — morning, afternoon or evenings. My working hours are flexible, but I'll give you an intense course and teach you how to make...' What? What would I teach Ruary to make?

No one had an immediate suggestion.

Marck had the first idea. 'An apron.'

Ruary screwed his face up.

'A gardener's apron,' Marck clarified. 'One of those sturdy, multi–pocketed jobs made from linen cotton canvas. You can stick your secateurs and whatever else you use in the pockets while you're wedding.'

'*Weeding*,' Ruary corrected him.

Marck blinked. He hadn't realised his slip–up.

'You said *wedding*,' Ruary enlightened him. 'Instead of *weeding*.'

Marck looked thoughtful. 'Did I? Whatever made me say that?'

Ruary glanced at me. 'I can't imagine.'

I brushed Marck's faux pas aside. 'You could sew curtains for your garden shed. I noticed you didn't have any curtains when I was there.'

Ruary didn't pull a face so I guessed that my suggestion had been received better than Marck's gardening apron idea.

'The shed would look pretty with curtains,' I added.

Ruary frowned. 'It's a shed. Does it need to look pretty?'

'Well, yes, why not?'

'Because it's a shed,' said Ruary.

I kept my pitch going. 'Curtains would be easier to sew as your first item.'

Marck intervened. 'An apron isn't difficult.'

'Yes, but it's got lots of pockets,' I argued. 'Pockets can be tricky, especially if Ruary has to mitre the corners.'

'Okay,' said Ruary. 'I'll go with the curtains.'

I smiled. 'Great. I'll pop round to your house to measure your size.'

Jannet almost choked on the cherry on her fairy cake and several women guffawed.

Sharla giggled and whispered to Denice. 'I bet Ruary's not short on size.' She gave a naughty wink.

Denice dug an elbow into her ribs but Sharla couldn't stop giggling.

Ruary's attitude brightened at the thought that I'd have to go to his house. He seemed happy to let me measure whatever I wanted.

'Or you could measure the window yourself,' I told him, 'and estimate how much fabric you need.'

'As long as he includes the seam allowance,' Jannet added.

'What's that?' Ruary asked.

'I'll pop over and measure the window,' I said, realising it would be easier.

So that was agreed.

'He'll have to make more than a pair of shed curtains,' said Marck.

I wasn't sure if he was trying to stir things up but he was right.

A quilt, a stuffed robin soft toy, a chocolate daisy pincushion and a gardening bag were some of the things we considered.

'A quilt is too large a task for a complete sewing novice,' said Marck.

Jannet had an idea. 'Ruary could make a quilt block. One piece of a quilt. It could have a flower, like an old–fashioned tea rose or bluebell on it as a nod to his vintage gardening work.'

'That's not a bad idea,' said Marck.

And so a floral quilt block was thrown into the mix. I had plenty of floral templates so I planned to use one of those to teach Ruary how to make the quilting piece.

Marck looked thoughtful. 'It's a shame he doesn't have the skill to make a gent's shirt. That would've impressed them.'

Ruary looked at me. 'Is a shirt too difficult?'

'It's one of the hardest items to make. A well-tailored man's shirt takes a lot of skill. The collar is very difficult.'

'Yes, but you could teach me,' said Ruary, suddenly wanting to challenge Marck's assumption that he wouldn't be able to do it.

'A granddad shirt,' I said. 'It doesn't have a full collar. I could show you how to make that if you're up for it.'

'Yes, I am.'

Marck's lips formed into a tight smile. He sighed heavily. 'I can give you shirt fabric. What colour of shirt would you like? And avoid pinstripes because matching the stripes would be a nightmare. Go for something plain but classy.'

'I'll leave it up to you, Marck,' he said. 'You're the expert.'

Marck nodded. 'I'll sort that out for you.'

I noted down what we'd agreed to make. 'Shed curtains...that covers home decor. A floral quilt block...to demonstrate that you're able to quilt. A gent's shirt...an item of clothing that's considered difficult to make. That should be enough to start with.'

'Are you going to help us make the dresses for the fashion show?' Denice asked Marck. 'Morag says we have to try and coordinate them with your menswear.'

'Yes, I'll certainly help, Denice. We'll all work together and put on a great show. Ruary can help to make the dresses. That will cover the fashion aspect. We'll photograph him doing this and put the pictures up on my website and his website,' said Marck.

Outnumbered by lots of women smiling at him, Ruary couldn't refuse. 'Dressmaking,' I heard him mutter as Jannet and I went through to the kitchen to make fresh tea. 'Whatever have I got myself into?'

The sewing bee finished around six, as I'd expected. The women left with their new dress fabrics and copies of the dress patterns that Violet had included.

'I'm going to cut out my fabric pieces tonight and make a start on my cocktail dress,' Jannet said to me. She was one of the last to leave. 'I'll let you know how I get on.'

I waved her off, and then turned to find Marck standing behind me.

'I'll choose a suitable shirt fabric for Ruary and drop that off to you tomorrow,' he said. 'I've also got a pattern for a classic granddad shirt that you can use.'

I smiled up at him. 'Great.'

Ruary lingered in the living room. Marck glanced at him and then said to me, 'See you tomorrow.'

I closed the door after Marck drove off and went through to the living room. Ruary wasn't there. He was in the shed getting ready to plant the chocolate daisies. I went out to chat to him. 'Is there anything you need?'

He rolled up his shirt sleeves. 'You could fill the watering can up for me while I plant these. They'll need regular watering especially on sunny days when the soil is dry. Don't drown them, just make sure they get watered regularly.'

'I will.'

I filled the watering can in the kitchen and carried it out to him. I put it down beside him on the lawn. 'I can smell the chocolate daisies from here. I told Zinnia that you were going to add them to the garden.'

'Yes, I know. She told me. She phoned me a couple of days ago to chat about...things.' He sounded deliberately vague.

'What things?'

'Gardening things, cottage things, romantic things.'

'Romantic?'

He continued to sort the daisies and didn't look up at me as he said, 'You and Marck, skinny–dipping in the sea.'

'We didn't. He wore swimming trunks and I wore one of his shirts over my...my undies.'

'Sounds like you had fun. Jannet mentioned that you were snogging. Definitely sounds like fun.'

'Not that it's any of your business, Ruary, we may have had a mild flirtation but nothing happened and we're just friends.'

'Very friendly.'

I stomped off into the house.

'I'll stick a couple of the chocolate daisies beside the thrift and candyfloss,' he called after me. 'They'll get plenty of sunshine there.'

'Stick them wherever you want,' I shouted and then muttered in annoyance. 'You can stick them where the sun doesn't shine for all I care.'

'I heard that.'

I sat down at my sewing machine and flicked through my new patterns, trying to concentrate on them until Ruary had gone. I half hoped he'd exit via the garden wall but he came ambling into the living room wondering how welcome he was.

'That's the flowers planted.'

'Thank–you. I'll tell Zinnia, or perhaps I'll leave that up to you considering that you keep in touch.'

He took my grumbling accusations on the chin and didn't argue.

'What are you doing tonight?' he said.

'Sitting here until the wee small hours working on my designs.'

He nodded and headed out of the lounge into the hallway.

'Why do you ask?'

He paused. 'Because I was hoping to do a trade with you. As I'm already here, it seems sensible to have a sewing lesson rather than come back tomorrow morning. I could come back tomorrow, but maybe in the afternoon. I have to reseed a chamomile lawn tomorrow.'

'What sort of trade?'

'While you continue working,' he motioned towards my patterns and artwork, 'I'll cook dinner for us. I'll serve it up, clear everything away, and then you can teach me how to...whatever it is I have to learn.'

It made sense. The ladies had already cleared everything away. Every cup and saucer was washed, dried and put in the cupboards. I was glad because the trip to Cornwall, London and Paris and then all the furore with the fashion show...well, my energy needle was in danger of hitting the empty mark.

He walked past me, back into the living room and through to the kitchen. I heard him rummaging around in the cupboards and fridge. 'When did you last do any food shopping?'

'Erm...I bought fresh bread and more milk and sugar for the sewing bee from the local shop.'

'What about food? The cupboards have got tumbleweeds blowing through them.'

'I used up the rest of my flour, butter and eggs baking cakes and scones today.'

'There are no vegetables, no fruit, no —' He cut short his list. 'I'll be back soon.'

And so the modern–day hunter–gatherer drove off to hit the supermarket and came back loaded with fresh vegetables, fruit, bread, rice, pasta and some frozen stuff which I didn't have time to see because he was whizzing around putting everything away and then washing his hands to start making dinner.

'Back to the grind, Morag.'

I took the hint to get on with my designs and let him rustle up a meal. Within minutes the aroma of onions, lemons, peppers and savoury paella came wafting through to the living room.

We ate dinner in the kitchen and I thanked him for making such a delicious meal.

We didn't talk about Marck, or Cornwall or Zinnia. Instead we discussed what I'd teach him to sew that evening.

After dinner we went through and I showed him how to thread up the sewing machine and let him try his hand at sewing spare pieces of fabric to get the feel of the machine. Within ten minutes he was sewing straight lines and could use the reverse button to finish off his stitches.

'You pick things up fast,' I said.

We sat together at the sewing machines and sometimes I felt my senses react when he leaned close to see what to do. Unless I was mistaken, I sensed a similar reaction from him.

He continued to practise on fabric scraps for the next hour, stopping only to make us tea, while I pushed ahead with my work.

'Can I come back tomorrow afternoon? Or would the evening be better for you?'

'Probably the afternoon. Or I could come over to your house and measure the shed window for the curtains.'

'That's going to interrupt your day.' He checked the time. 'It's not that late. Do you want to drive over with me now? We could be there and back in less than an hour.'

He wanted to drive me over, but I took my own car and followed him so that he didn't need to drive me home again.

He flicked on the garden lights and the lamp inside the shed. The path was lit with solar lights.

Inside the shed I stood up on a box and used the measuring tape I'd brought with me to measure the length and depth of the window. I jotted down the figures. 'Would you be able to put up hooks on either side of the window for hanging the curtains?'

'Yes, I'll sort that out.'

He helped me climb down and I found myself wrapped in his strong arms, inches from his handsome face, gazing into those blue eyes of his.

Maybe I was tired, perhaps I was feeling in a crazy–wild mood, or was I just reacting as many women would to a handsome man whose lips were a breath away from kissing her? Ruary kissed me and I didn't resist. I returned his passion and then...I pulled away.

Ruary still held me close. 'What's wrong, Morag?' he said softly.

I gazed up at him and he knew what was wrong without me having to tell him.

He gently let me go and gave a resigned smile. 'Marck.'

'I have to go. I'll have fabrics that you can choose from tomorrow for the curtains. Come over as agreed and I'll teach you how to sew them.'

I hurried out, almost dropping my measuring tape as I fumbled in my bag for my car keys.

Ruary ran after me. 'You don't have to run away, Morag.'

I gave him an anxious smile and nodded though I didn't agree. I did have to run away. Tonight I could've ended up getting involved with Ruary. He'd made his interest clear. But something in my heart held me back from taking things further. I wanted to get back to the cottage.

'See you tomorrow,' I said to him and then I drove off.

I couldn't settle and snuggled up on the sofa thinking about everything that had happened. I thought about Marck and Cornwall. Maybe I shouldn't have gone there. I still hadn't had a chance to relax at the cottage which had been what I'd planned to do when I moved in. Apart from the Wednesday sewing bee, the rest of the time I was free to enjoy the comfy cottage, sew, bake cakes, enjoy the garden and get on with my designs. Instead I'd been dashing off with Marck, getting involved in the fashion show, appeared on television, and was now responsible for teaching Ruary to sew. And it was only Wednesday.

I padded over to my work table and tidied away some of my designs. That's when I remembered that I'd promised to email some quilt block patterns to Violet and Zinnia. Realising I'd totally forgotten in all melee of things that had happened, I opened up my laptop, scanned in the patterns and then emailed them off to Zinnia whose email was the first one I found in my purse.

I continued to sort out my designs and searched through my fabric stash for a metre of fabric that would be suitable for the shed's curtains. One metre was enough to make a pair. I saw a cornflower and pansy print that I thought I'd show Ruary, along with another two vintage–style floral prints.

Then I heard an email ping on my laptop that I'd left open on the table. I checked to see who it was from and was surprised to find a reply from Zinnia. I opened the mail and read the message: 'Thanks, Morag. These will make lovely quilt blocks. Love, Zinnia.'

I typed a reply. 'It's two o'clock in the morning.'

She replied. 'I couldn't sleep.'

'Neither could I.'

'Thinking about Marck? Or Ruary?'

How did she know?

'Something like that. Thinking about Marck and our time in Cornwall. Miss him, you, Violet, everything.'

'You need time for things in your life, especially your romantic life, to settle, Morag.'

'You're right.'

'Has Ruary kissed you yet?'

Was there any point in lying? I didn't think so.

'Yes. He kissed me tonight when I was measuring his shed window for curtains.'

'A floral pattern would be nice.'

'I've got a cornflower and pansy print and two vintage florals.'

'They all sound lovely.'

'Did Ruary phone you tonight?' I asked her.

'No, I phoned him on Monday but we haven't chatted since then. I may have let slip about you and Marck.'

'Yes, the skinny dipping. And Jannet told him about the snogging.'

'What snogging? Did Marck kiss you in Cornwall?'

Shit!

'He did, yes. Once. We've put it aside,' I replied.

'That's a shame. Never mind. Let me know what fabric you choose for the shed. Remember, ribbon or bias binding are ideal for tiebacks and trims. I'd better let you get some sleep. I'll do the same. But could you remind Ruary to air the tent?'

'What tent?'

'The one that's in my shed. I'll need it when Violet and I come up to Glasgow for Marck's fashion show. We're staying overnight.'

'At the cottage? I'll book into a bed and breakfast.'

'Don't talk nonsense, Morag. You're living in the cottage. Violet and I used to love camping out in the tent in the garden during the summer. It'll be June.'

'I'll book you into a hotel. Or you could have a sleepover at Marck's house.' Wherever that was in Glasgow. All I knew was that he had a well–trimmed hedge. 'You can't rough it in a tent in the garden, Zinnia.'

'It'll be an adventure. We used to love it. We've even got an oil lamp. Night, night.'

And that was it.

I closed the laptop and got ready for bed. Before turning the living room lights off I scribbled a note for myself to remember to tell Ruary to air the tent. Not that I could forget that easily. Air the tent and choose your floral fabric. Yes, another hectic day lay ahead.

Chapter Twelve

Sewing & Baking Cakes

I was making breakfast when Marck arrived with the shirt fabric. It was a traditional cream coloured fabric and expensive looking. He'd also brought a pattern for a granddad shirt in a medium size.

He put them down beside my sewing machine and then followed me through to the kitchen. I had a pot of porridge cooking on the stove. I gave it a stir. It was ready.

'Porridge? That looks yummy. I haven't had porridge in ages.'

'Would you like a bowl?'

He sat down at the kitchen table while I spooned out two bowls of porridge from the pot. He helped himself to creamy milk.

I poured our tea.

'I like the shirt fabric,' I said.

'When is Ruary's first lesson, or did he have one from you last night?'

'He did, and he's dropping by this afternoon for another lesson. I went over to his house last night to measure the window of the shed. We'll make a start on the curtains. It'll give him a chance to machine along the hems and get a feel for the sewing. Then we'll tackle the shirt and the quilting.'

'If you need a hand with the shirt, let me know. You'll probably have to alter the waistline. Ruary's got a strapping build. The shoulders on the granddad shirt are generous so they should fit him, but he's got a trim waist so you'll have to alter that to fit him. And remember to take photographs of him sewing.'

'I've got my camera ready.'

I poured more tea and tried not to feel guilty about kissing Ruary. It wasn't as if Marck and I were planning to be more than friends. We'd both date other people.

'Zinnia emailed me late last night. Neither of us could sleep and I emailed the patterns I'd promised her and we ended up chatting via email. She wants me to remind Ruary to air the tent from the shed. She's planning on sleeping in the tent, with Violet, when they're up for your fashion show.'

He sipped his tea. 'Yes, it'll need airing.'

'You're okay about Zinnia and Violet camping out in the garden?'

'They love that tent. I'd never approve if it was winter or early spring when it rains. June should be lovely. I think they've even got an oil lamp.'

'I thought perhaps you'd invite them to sleepover at your house. I've no idea where you live but I assume it's in the city.'

'It is. My house is in the same area as Ruary's house.'

'One of the large mansions?'

'With a large garden and a shed.'

'You've got a shed?'

'Yes. Do I sense some sort of shed envy from you?'

'No, no, well...maybe...'

I explained that I'd invariably lived in a flat and often longed for a garden. A shed was part of that. One of those sheds where I could sew and paint, knit and sketch. A creative shed painted in pastel colours and with a vintage decor.

'You've got the use of Zinnia's shed for the summer. I don't think she'd want you to paint it, but you're welcome to bring your paint pots and set about painting mine. I only had it put up a few months ago.'

'Thanks, but it would be something else that I'd have to give up at the end of the summer. I know I'm going to miss the cottage. I could paint your shed and then have to give it back to you when the summer lease of the cottage is complete.'

'Consider it your shed. We're going to stay friends, aren't we, even when Zinnia comes back to her cottage and you go to live wherever?'

'In another flat in Glasgow.' After kissing Ruary I doubted I'd move in with him.

'Probably, but you won't be leaving the city, will you? You'll still be able to come and enjoy the shed, *your shed*. If you lived in a flat again it would be particularly beneficial. A little niche, painted eau–de–nil or pale blue, a sewing shed, where you could make more patterns and earn enough not to live in a flat.'

I was tempted. A shed. I'd always wanted a shed. A sewing and painting shed.

'The shed has only one key. I'd give it to you. I promise I wouldn't snoop around and try to see if you'd designed anything that would be suitable for my menswear.'

'I'd have the key?'

He nodded firmly. 'And I'm rubbish at picking locks.'

Ruary arrived at the cottage mid–afternoon. I'd been sewing and baking cakes. I put the kettle on for tea and offered him a slice of lemon drizzle cake.

He leaned against the edge of the kitchen doorway. 'That would be great. Did you bake it?'

I cut two slices. 'Yes, using the flour, eggs and fresh lemons you bought.'

I put the tea and cake on a tray and carried it through to the living room.

I pointed to the fabric beside the sewing machines. 'Marck dropped off the shirt fabric and a pattern for you.'

Ruary lifted up the pattern. 'This looks difficult to make, but I like it — and the fabric is classy. I thought perhaps Marck would screw with me and select something garish.'

'Why would he want to do that?'

Ruary's blue eyes held me in their gaze. He shrugged his broad shoulders and my stomach tightened the way it had before when I was near him.

'We'll have our tea and cake and then get started.' I handed him a slice of cake on a vintage plate and a napkin. 'Lemon drizzle cake and expensive cream shirt fabric don't mix well.'

He was careful not to mark the fabric as he bit into his cake. 'Mmm, this is scrumptious. You're an excellent baker.'

'I love sewing and baking.'

He smiled at me and I felt a flurry of excitement. I got up and started to prepare the shirt fabric. I put it on Zinnia's fold–away cutting table that I'd set up in the living room near the sewing machines.

I showed him how to fold the fabric according to the pattern layout. Then we cut out the pattern pieces and pinned them on to the fabric. I snapped photographs of Ruary working on each stage of the process.

He read the instructions on the pattern pieces. 'This makes common sense. Two front pieces. One back piece. Two sleeves, two cuffs, and two pieces for the front and back of the granddad collar.'

'Some shirts have shoulder pieces but this is quite a basic pattern. It's still difficult to make but if you can grasp how the pieces fit together then we can start to pin it ready to sew the first seams.'

We pinned the front and back pieces together, and then I let him put the thread in his machine and set it up. He remembered what I'd shown him the previous night.

'Okay, put the presser foot down and lower the needle so that it's in the fabric ready for the first stitch. Then put your foot on the pedal to start sewing.'

I went through all the things he needed to do, including using the edge marker on the sewing machine so that the seam edges were straight. This made it easier for him to sew. Thankfully, Marck had given us plenty of fabric so if things went wonky we could cut out another pattern.

However, we didn't need to. Ruary turned out to be adept at using the sewing machine. The things he'd learned the previous night had really helped. He'd grasped the basics of how to sew. During the next three hours he learned how to do back stitches at the start and finish of his seams to secure the threads and various basic sewing techniques. He even managed to make the buttonholes on the front of the shirt.

I continued to take photographs. This was working well. Ruary was working well. In fact, if he could learn how to top stitch the shirt he'd be able to finish it. With my help of course.

'You're really suited to this,' I said to him. 'You've got nimble fingers and steady hands.'

He smiled at me. 'Gardening work. You need strength for the heavy tasks like cutting down branches, but careful hands for handling the seedlings. They're tiny, fragile. Sometimes each seed has to be planted individually, especially for the rarer flowers.'

'Well, it's given you a distinct advantage for the sewing. You'll be able to tackle the quilt blocks soon. Seeing how you've handled the shirt, I'm sure you'll be making up a quilt next.'

The shirt was half finished.

'Should I try it on?' he said.

'Eh, yes. If it fits across the chest but needs darts to taper the waistline we'll add those before fitting the sleeves in.'

Ruary unbuttoned his shirt. He wore jeans and I felt the need to look away and concentrated on my sewing machine while he undressed.

'You can look now.'

'I was just...'

He smiled at me.

I had my hair tied back in a ponytail and felt him look at me closely as I checked that the shirt fitted okay. It did. I walked around him, fussing with the fabric. 'We could put a couple of darts into the back but I think the granddad style works well being loose.'

'Feels a fine fit to me.' He put his hands on my shoulders and smiled down at me. His broad shoulders blocked out the light shining in the cottage window. 'Thanks for teaching me to sew, Morag. I appreciate you taking the time to do this. I know you have your own work to do. And I'm sorry that I kissed you last night.'

I let my gaze fall to his chest. His golden, tanned torso was visible between the gap in the shirt that had yet to have the buttons sewn on. It hung open, revealing a smooth chest that reminded me of Marck's physique. They were so similar in build, except perhaps for Ruary's extra broad shoulders but this shirt would've fitted Marck. That's when I realised that even standing within a breath of temptation, I thought about Marck while being this close to Ruary.

I nodded. 'Me too. Let's put it behind us. It was just one of those moments. I don't want there to be any awkwardness.'

'I won't kiss you again,' he promised, though the words didn't seem to come easy to him. 'Unless you ask me to.'

I brushed the stray strands of hair back from my face. 'Okay, let's push on with this shirt.'

'Ruary's finished the shirt?' Marck sounded less than pleased when I phoned to tell him.

'You sound jealous that he's picked it up so fast. But he has a knack for sewing. He's ended up doing a great job of the shirt. I thought you'd be pleased that the fabric and the pattern worked.'

'I'm not jealous, just a trifle peeved. What's the top stitching like on the collar and cuffs?'

'Tidy. I showed him how to use the machine to keep the stitching nice and straight. What can I say? He's got a bloomin' knack for sewing. He's got strong hands and nimble fingers.'

'Has he indeed?'

I ignored Marck's attitude. 'He's coming round tomorrow to learn how to make quilt blocks and finish the curtains for the shed.'

'Maybe you should get him to help you whip up your dress for the fashion show while he's there.'

'I'll do that,' I snapped at him.

'Are we having a tiff?'

'Yes.'

'Okay then. I'll call in a couple of days when we're not annoyed with each other.'

'I'm not annoyed with you,' I snipped at him.

'That's a lie.'

'Okay, I'm a bit annoyed with you. You're being silly because Ruary has made the shirt.'

'That's not entirely the reason.'

'What's the part that's missing?' I said.

'I promised not to say.'

'Tell me.'

'No,' he said firmly.

'Goodnight, Marck.' I hung up on him.

Three days passed without either of us phoning the other. I was amazed by the amount of work that I got done. Very little. I kept rewinding our conversation. What was Marck not telling me? And why I so upset that we'd had our first proper falling out?

Chapter Thirteen

Tea Dresses & Busy Bees

Ruary came round at eight in the evening to learn how to satin stitch the edges of a teacup appliqué on a quilt block. He brought a bottle of wine with him.

'We're celebrating,' he announced, holding up the bottle.

'I've made fresh lemonade. I used up the bag of lemons you bought before they went squishy.'

He put the bottle down. 'Lemonade it is.'

He followed me through to the kitchen where I poured two tall glasses of lemonade.

'What are we celebrating?' I said.

'I bought a sewing machine.'

'Really?'

'It's similar to the one I've been sewing with here, only it's the latest model. According to the sales staff, when I showed them a photograph of me using your machine, they said it's got more embroidery features, stitches and stuff.' He smiled. 'And...I bought something else with it. It was sort of a deal. A bargain.'

'What else did you buy?'

'An overlocking machine.'

Even I didn't have one of those. Wanted one, yes, but didn't have one.

'I've got it in the car. I wondered if the ladies would like to use it to make their dresses. The shop said it's used to stitch the edges of seams. And they can sew rolled hems.'

He brought both machines in and we set them up on the table. I photographed Ruary using the machines.

'You definitely look like a sewist now, Ruary.'

That evening, he made his first quilt block and finished sewing the floral curtains for his shed.

Jannet phoned late on Monday night. The new class that she'd set up for those interested in our sewing bee had been busy. Denice and Sharla had helped out. They planned to keep the class running during the summer.

I told her about Ruary's success with sewing.

'Encourage him to model his new granddad shirt on Wednesday at the bee. The ladies will love to fondle his buttons for him.'

'You're scandalous, Jannet.'

She laughed. 'Me? You're the one he was kissing.'

I sighed.

'There's no chance of keeping things like that quiet when you're surrounded by people like us, Morag.'

I managed to avoid further scandal until the Wednesday sewing bee. Ruary arrived early and set about making another quilt block. He wore his granddad shirt, as requested.

'Would you like a cup of tea?' I said. 'And I've baked fruit scones and shortbread.'

'Tea and a piece of shortbread, thanks.'

The women started to arrive. While I made the tea, Ruary let them in. I heard Jannet and Denice's voices as they encouraged Ruary to model his shirt. He drew the line at walking up and down the living room but let the women have a feel of the fabric.

'Can I see how you stitched the inside seams?' Sharla asked him.

He unbuttoned his shirt.

I don't know who gave a wolf whistle but Denice looked shamefaced.

Any interest in the scones, shortbread or the cakes that they'd brought was cast aside to get close to Ruary's chest.

And of course that's when Marck arrived. Someone had left the front door open and he walked into the living room to find Ruary surrounded by the ladies. Marck glared at me. I pretended not to notice.

'Fairy cake, Marck?' I offered brightly.

'That would be lovely, Morag.' He went over to Ruary. 'So this is the shirt?'

The women stood back and Ruary let him study the shirt. 'I suppose you're going to say it's shoddy.'

'No, it's not. It's an excellent shirt,' said Marck.

I put a fairy cake on a plate for Marck and poured him a cup of tea. I watched the tension between him and Ruary.

Marck turned and smiled at me. 'You've taught him well.'

'All the seams are overlocked,' said Sharla. 'Have you got an overlocking machine?' she asked me.

I explained about Ruary buying a sewing machine and an overlocking machine.

'Ruary's offered to leave the overlocking machine here so that we can use it to make the dresses,' I added.

The women cheered and there was a flurry of excitement as they started to bring out the dresses they'd been working on for the past week. Some of them, like Jannet and Denice, had made great progress, while others were still working with the pattern pieces.

'I wasn't sure how to cut the skirt on my dress but I've been working on the bodice,' said Sharla.

Some of the women offered to help her and I suggested they spread the pink silk fabric and organza out on the cutting table.

While they were busy, two other ladies used the overlocking machine to sew the hems on their silk and chiffon dresses.

I went over to Marck and Ruary.

'I was just telling Ruary that he should have no problem with the press interviews now. His sewing skills are excellent.'

Ruary put his arm casually around my shoulder, as if he was used to doing this, and gave me a squeeze. 'I couldn't have done it without Morag. All the late nights she worked with me, teaching me everything I needed to know. I have her to thank.'

I saw a flicker of hurt in Marck's eyes. 'Well, I really can't stay any longer this afternoon. I'm busy organising the show.' He spoke up so the women could hear him. 'The dress rehearsal for the fashion show is next Wednesday night. Can you all make it along?' He gave them details of the time and the hotel function suite.

An atmosphere of excitement filled the cottage. Everyone agreed to be there.

'Bring your dresses,' said Marck. 'Even if they're not completely finished, you'll have to wear them so that we can see how they fit in with the menswear. Then you'll have another few days to sew them. The show is on next Saturday.' He smiled at Ruary. 'You're invited of course. Wear your shirt. I'll give you a waistcoat to wear with it.'

Ruary agreed to do this.

'I'll see myself out,' said Marck. As he left, the cottage buzzed with the dressmaking activity.

Denice brought her purple dress over to Ruary. She held it up. 'What do you think?'

I think I heard him say that the dress was lovely, but the sounds around me drifted as I watched out the front window of the cottage. I saw Marck get into his car and drive off. He didn't even glance back.

The next week was hectic, trying to find time to make my dress for the fashion show along with my other work.

Ruary went ahead with his press interview, inviting them to his house where he'd set up the sewing machine and the overlocker. He promised to have the overlocker back in time for the sewing bee. And he did. Over afternoon tea he told us that the interview went fine, and that they'd taken photographs of him sewing.

'What did you sew?' Jannet asked him.

'A quilt block. I also showed them the shirt I'd made and the curtains. They were well impressed. I've another interview with a magazine but I'll just do what I did and it should be okay.'

Jannet put her gold dress on the mannequin and made a few adjustments. All the women had finished their dresses. They'd helped each other, and I'd helped too. The dress rehearsal was later that evening.

My turquoise dress was finished. The ladies had helped me with the fittings. I planned to wear it with a pair of court shoes that I'd covered with spare pieces of the fabric to match the dress.

'Oh that's fantastic, Morag,' said Jannet. 'I wish I'd covered my shoes to match.'

Several of them wanted to do this so I showed them an easy way to attach the fabric. They wouldn't have the shoes ready for the dress rehearsal but they'd have them finished for the actual show.

I'd invited them to bring their dresses, shoes and accessories with them to the Wednesday bee and then come back in time for us to head to the hotel. Marck had arranged a mini–bus to take us all there. His phone call to me was friendly but different from before. Something had changed between us. I think that was due to Ruary.

I hadn't seen Marck since the previous sewing bee, and although Ruary had dropped by a couple of times, he'd been busy with his gardening work and media interviews. So I'd had time to work on my designs — and I'd been out on my vintage bike cycling around Glasgow.

After everyone left that afternoon, heading home to have dinner, sort their hair and get ready for the dress rehearsal, I cycled through the city centre in the mellow sunlight. I was back at the cottage in time to put on some makeup.

The ladies arrived at the cottage that evening in a flurry of excitement and we set off in the mini-bus to the hotel function suite. Ruary said he'd drive there himself.

The lighting men and other assistants were setting up the stage and runway. It was a lot more glamorous than I'd thought. Marck was in the centre of everything, directing where he wanted the models to stand, asking that the lighting be adjusted to focus on certain aspects of the show and generally pulling the whole thing together.

He nodded and smiled when he saw me but he didn't come over. The distance between us felt friendly and yet...the closeness had gone.

The two changing rooms behind the stage area were jumping with activity. The ladies changing room was filled with laughter, gossip and giggling as we put on our dresses.

The male models sounded just as lively, and I could hear Marck telling them how he wanted them to present the clothes. Then he called through to us. 'Are you ready, ladies?'

We went out on to the stage and were paired up with the male models. Ruary was one of them. He wore a waistcoat and dark trousers with his granddad shirt. He'd swept his hair back and fitted in well with the models.

I waited to see who Marck would pair me with.

'Your dress is beautiful,' Marck said to me. 'All the ladies have done a fine job with their dresses. I think you'll look great walking down the runway with Ruary.'

Ruary was delighted with this. I wasn't sure. Yes, I was comfortable to partner up with Ruary but I wondered why Marck now seemed to want us to be together.

I didn't ask him and Marck hurried on, organising the rehearsal.

The function room lights were dimmed and spotlights lit up the stage area. Jannet's gold dress was gorgeous and she'd covered her shoes to match. It was quite an outfit. The cocktail-length dress had a figure-flattering shape, and Jannet had terrific legs. She usually had them covered but tonight they were on display in the glitzy gold dress. She walked down the runway with a handsome chap whose antique gold fabric waistcoat bore the zinnia design.

Next up was Denice. Her purple dress was stunning and so was Denice. She wasn't tall or model–like but she was a lovely–looking woman. Marck had paired her with a male model wearing a waistcoat and tie in purple tones.

Sharla's pink dress was a confection in itself and she walked down the runway with a male model whose pink pinstripe shirt was the perfect match for her. I recognised the pink silk on the back of his waistcoat. It was the zinnia fabric that Marck had given to his aunt when we were in Cornwall. The design worked well.

The women put on a great show. No one stumbled. The sewing bee ladies dresses were ideal for the fashion show. Some of the women had also made a bolero and Jannet had sewn a velvet cloak.

The final couple took to the stage. It was Ruary and me. He linked my arm through his and we walked down together to the front of the runway, paused as we'd been instructed by one of Marck's assistants, and then walked back up to the stage. Ruary's waistcoat was cream on the front and had blue silk on the back. My turquoise dress was a vintage shift design that skimmed my figure and shimmered under the lights.

The rehearsal went well. Marck thanked everyone and told them to be back for the show on Saturday evening.

The mini–bus dropped the ladies off at their respective houses and finally dropped me off at the cottage. I hadn't had a moment to speak to Ruary after we'd been on stage because the bus was waiting to take us home. Marck had waved to me from the stage area as we left.

The bus dropped me off at the cottage. I went inside, made a cup of tea, hung my dress up, put my shoes in a bag so that they were ready for the show on Saturday, and went to bed.

During the next few days everyone seemed busy with their own lives, as I was with mine, getting on with my work until it was time for show.

Marck's fashion show was a success. The press were there, buyers, clients, customers, friends. The hotel function suite was packed. I enjoyed being one of the models and had a great time with Jannet and the others.

Zinnia and Violet had to cancel their trip to Glasgow due to a fiasco at their shop in Cornwall. They promised to come up and visit later in the summer. And they still wanted to stay overnight in the tent.

Craig and his cameraman turned up to film part of the show and included the ladies from the sewing bee. He said it was going to air as a follow–up feature.

Quite a few of those involved were going for a meal after the show to celebrate. Marck was so swept up in everything that I barely had a chance to chat to him. Again, he was polite but distant. Ruary was going to the meal, but I just wanted to go back to the cottage.

Ruary told me to keep the overlocking machine at the cottage so the sewing bee ladies could use it during the summer. And if I decided to come and stay at his house after the cottage lease was finished, I could bring it with me.

Jannet and Denice came hurrying over to me as I headed out of the hotel. I'd changed into my casual clothes and had my dress and shoes in a bag. The mini–bus was waiting to take a number of them to the meal, so I planned to take a taxi home. I'd phoned and one was due to arrive within minutes.

Jannet's voice was filled with enthusiasm. 'We've got a double date,' she said to me.

I smiled at her. 'A date?'

'Yes, two of the lighting engineers from the fashion show have asked Denice and me to go out with them.'

Denice squealed with glee. 'I haven't had a date since Christmas. It shows you what an evening dress can do for you.'

'Have a great time,' I told them, and we all gave each other a hug before I jumped in the taxi.

I gazed out the window as the taxi drove through the city. The twilight sky was lit with an amber and lilac glow. I rolled down the window and breathed in the warm night air. I felt as if I was on my own, but I was okay with that. Maybe that's what I needed — time to adjust to my new life and build a future from there.

June was a scorcher in the city. The first two weeks were hot and muggy. It rained twice but this refreshed the atmosphere and the streets dried quickly again as the temperatures soared. It was forecast to be one of the warmest summers in years.

Craig's follow–up feature was on the television and again there was increased interest in our sewing bee. Everyone seemed delighted with that. We even got a mention in a couple of the newspapers.

The Wednesday sewing bee continued as usual. Jannet and Denice were still dating the lighting engineers and seemed happy with their choices. The Monday night sewing classes were popular and Jannet had extended the classes to include some at her house. Denice had teamed up with her and they'd created a small business from this. Sharla had become involved and it seemed to be working well for all of them.

My routine settled into the one I'd assumed I'd have when I moved into the cottage. I had time to relax, enjoy the garden, work on my collections and plan what I wanted to do after the summer.

I got a lot of sewing done. I made pincushions with butterfly and teacup prints. I even made sew tidy books and sewing cases for Jannet and Denice who said they wanted them. I gave them as gifts, along with the patterns, and we continued to share templates and techniques during the sewing bee afternoons. One of the ladies showed us how to embroider vintage flowers from old fashioned patterns and Jannet taught us how to do needle turned appliqué. We all learned from each other. Friendships were forged. Friendships that would last.

Ruary came round once a fortnight to tend the cottage garden. He didn't kiss me but he flirted a bit. Summer was his busy time for the gardening work, but he kept up his sewing and joined in with the sewing bee whenever he could.

June became July so quickly. I felt fitter and stronger than I had when I first moved into the cottage. I rarely thought about Gavyn, but I wondered about Marck. I saw him sometimes when he popped into the sewing bee. He never waited long. Occasionally, he'd have a quick cup of tea but we didn't have any time alone together. He only came over when the other ladies were sewing.

Zinnia emailed once to ask if I was okay. She didn't ask about Marck, or whether we were getting on. I guessed she knew. Marck would've told her.

July was a busy month. The sewing bee was sometimes held outside in the garden. There were folding chairs and tables and large umbrellas in the shed. I put them out when the sun was scorching. It rained a fair bit in July but it was still warm. Sewing outside when it was dry was a pleasure and I found myself looking forward to Wednesday afternoons. The women made the sewing machine cover I designed. I made two covers for Zinnia's machines — a cottage and a floral print. Jannet made a cover with one of my patterns — a fabric print with vintage sewing machines, bees, butterflies, teacups and cakes.

I gave them more patterns for quilt blocks. Jannet pieced together a chocolate daisy quilt and included bumblebees.

I made myself a tea dress using a traditional pattern that was part of my collection. I wore it for afternoon tea during one of the sewing bees and when the others saw it they made tea dresses in various fabrics.

We made everything from patchwork fairy dolls and softie toys to bunting, knitted bumblebees, made vintage aprons, beehive pincushions, pattern weights, large sewing bags with teacup, cake and tea dress designs, and little cottage, shed and bakery quilts. We were very busy bees.

July gave way to August which was the driest month of the year. The hot summer evenings were wonderful for jumping on my bike and cycling through the city. I knew the weather would change soon so I made the most of the warm evenings when Glasgow shone in mellow tones of burnished bronze and golds. My new life in the cottage in the city suited me well.

Chapter Fourteen

Romantic Vintage

Jannet came round for lunch one day in August. We sat in the kitchen with the patio doors in the living room open to let the air waft in.

We chatted, and inevitably the conversation came round to Marck and Ruary.

'Marck's still keeping a polite distance,' I said.

'He's not the man for you though, is he?'

I shrugged and focussed on my tomato salad. 'I never really got a chance to find out. We had our moments. I thought we'd stay friends, but we're not close any more.'

'Marck liked you. That's why he let you go.'

I poured our tea.

'What about you and Ruary?' she said.

'I think he's waiting for me to move into his house when the lease finishes.'

'You know that you're welcome to stay with me until you find somewhere to live when you move out of the cottage. You'll not be stuck.'

'Thanks, Jannet. But I've had time to think and I suppose I'll lease the room and kitchen at Ruary's house. I like his garden and the thought of moving back into a flat makes my heart sink.'

'Ruary would be my choice. The man, the house, the life with him. You could settle with him.'

'Yes, but would I be settling for him?'

'Romance isn't always perfect, Morag. You've never given Ruary a proper chance. Any man who learns to sew to impress a woman is worth looking twice at.'

'He learned to sew because —'

'Because of the press and all that, yes, but also to get close to you. It nearly worked. He was never away from the cottage.'

'I didn't know that,' I told her.

'Do yourself a favour, broaden your horizons. Marck wasn't even a summer romance. Give Ruary a chance. Marck is a will–o'–the–wisp when it comes to love. He's not the settling down type.

Even he admits that. And that's why he's not interfering in your life. He's doing the right thing letting you get on with your own life.'

After Jannet left I kept thinking about the things she'd said. What if I'd made a mistake? What if the man for me was there all along?

I was knitting a bumblebee with yellow and chocolate brown wool when Ruary phoned.

'What are you up to this evening?' he said.

'Knitting a bumblebee.'

'Never a dull moment in your life, eh Morag?'

'This cottage is a hive of activity.'

'Could I tempt you away to have dinner with me at my house?'

'Maybe.'

'I'm on my way,' he said.

'No, I'll drive over.'

'I'll set the table for two. See you soon.'

I put on a tea dress, tidied my hair, freshened my makeup and drove over to Ruary's house.

He was in the kitchen wearing an apron. Dinner plates with a large helping of salad were on the table. No doubt the leafy lettuce, spring onions, tomatoes, baby carrots, radishes and chopped parsley were fresh from his garden.

'Take a seat. When the fish is cooked, our dinner is ready.' He dropped the first piece of fish dipped in batter into the pan, then a second piece. It fizzled as it cooked up light, crisp and golden. He shook the excess oil off and served it up.

We chatted about our work, and after dinner he showed me the part of the house that he leased out. The bedroom was decorated in dark blues and cream. The living room was neutral shades. The kitchen had a mix of colours and designs and was probably the room I liked the most. The bathroom had a bath with a shower. I pictured enjoying a leisurely bath instead of timing myself in the shower.

'What do you think?' he said.

'It's very comfortable. I like the decor.'

'Zinnia will be back in a few weeks,' he reminded me.

'Yes, I'd forgotten that you know more about her plans than me, and I live in the cottage.'

'The lease finishes in September. I know that's several weeks away but you should be starting to look for somewhere else to live now. Or you could try living here, some nights, to see if you like it. Then when Zinnia comes back you'd already be settled.'

'And she's definitely coming back? Marck mentioned that she'd been thinking of moving down to Cornwall.'

'Yes, she's coming back for at least another year.'

'I'm probably going to take you up on your offer to lease part of your house. I won't move in until I have to move out of the cottage. I couldn't afford to rent two houses.'

'There would be no charge. You wouldn't have to pay the lease on two properties. You could trying living here rent free to see if you want to move in.'

I smiled. 'I'm not sure.'

'Stay tonight.' He stepped close and wrapped his arms around me.

'You promised not to kiss me.'

'I was never any use at keeping promises.' He leaned down and kissed me.

I didn't resist.

Although it would've been easy to sleep with Ruary that night, I didn't. We kissed and snuggled close. I didn't want to take things further. I wasn't ready, so I drove home in the early hours of the morning.

I went over to have dinner at Ruary's house often, and we finally became very close. The intimacy we shared felt right. I'd given Ruary a chance.

September emerged so quickly, and when Zinnia arrived back in Glasgow, I'd already moved out and was living at Ruary's house.

The sewing bee was no longer part of my responsibility. But I intended going to the bee on Wednesday afternoons like all the others. It felt weird at first because I was so used to living in the cottage. It had become my home. Now it was Zinnia's home again. My home was with Ruary.

I'd sent off my two design collections. The company acknowledged that they liked the designs and paid me the other half of the money. Then I received an email from them at the end of September telling me that they wanted to commission me to design new patterns and another collection.

I jumped up and down and ran through to tell Ruary the exciting news.

'Do you have to design another collection?' His tone flattened the sparkle out of me. He was working in his study, deciding whether to add cosmos flowers to his new range of seed packets.

'I want to design it. It's my business, my career. It's how I make a living, Ruary.'

'But I've got money. You don't have to work. I have more than enough money to look after you.'

'Well that's great, but I like to be able to look after myself.'

'Why do you have to make things difficult for yourself, and for me?'

'I have to go. I'm going to be late for the sewing bee.'

I hadn't seen Marck in a long time so when I saw him walk into the cottage that afternoon I wasn't ready for the effect he had on me. He looked well, fit, strong, capable. I felt myself smile when I saw him. He smiled back at me and came over, took my hands in his and kissed them.

'It's lovely to see you again, Morag. How are things with you?'

I told him about the email offering me another contact for my patterns and designs.

'That's great. How fast did you type your reply?' He pretended to add up the letters required. 'How long did it take you to type — hell yes?'

I laughed.

'Well done. I'm sure it'll be a brilliant collection.'

'I eh...I haven't replied yet. I haven't said yes. Not yet.'

'Why not?'

I explained about what happened with Ruary.

'That's ridiculous. He has no business curtailing your business. Never let any man do that to you. Send that email and tell them yes before they change their minds and offer the contract to someone else. Someone who doesn't have a wet blanket like Ruary making them feel guilty for wanting to get on with their work.'

I went out into the garden and accessed my email on my phone. Then I typed a brief reply that basically said, 'Yes, I'd love to do it. Send the contract. I'll sign it. And thanks again.'

Ruary didn't approve. He blamed Marck for interfering. We had an enormous row and I packed my bags. I put them in the car and drove off.

I needed somewhere to stay for a few nights until I found somewhere else to live. I thought about booking into a hotel. I considered going to Jannet's house. She'd offered to put me up but her boyfriend stayed overnight quite often. I didn't want to intrude and ruin things for them. Then I thought of somewhere else...

'It's a safety lamp, Morag. The tent won't go on fire.'

Zinnia erected the tent in minutes.

She'd offered to let me sleep on one of the sofas but I didn't want to crease the chintz. Besides, the tent had aired for weeks. Zinnia assured me that it had no creepy–crawlies.

I zipped myself into a sleeping bag. 'Thanks for doing this.'

'I'm glad to have the company,' said Zinnia. 'It'll be nice to have breakfast with someone. Mornings are the worst time for me. That's when I realise I'm on my own. Once the day gets started and I get into my sewing and baking I don't think about it because I'm too busy and later I'm too tired. I miss Violet, so I'm happy to have you here at the cottage.'

It didn't take long for Marck to hear what had happened. Zinnia made my breakfast and we were only on our second cup of tea when he arrived at the cottage.

He exchanged a look with Zinnia. She'd phoned him. I knew she would.

'I'm just going to drink my tea out on the patio.' She smiled at me and left us to chat.

He wore an immaculate grey suit, shirt, waistcoat and tie. He looked like he'd recently jumped in the shower and trounced my time. His eyes were bright and yet the blue–green flashed with doubt, a hint of nervousness.

'Is there something wrong?' I asked him. I sat at the table cupping my tea.

'Yes.'

'What is it?'

'Everything. Everything's wrong. I messed up big style with you. I shouldn't have stepped back and let you go. That was a huge mistake. It was all my fault. But I've had time to think things over, and I've come here to win you back.'

Win me back?

He continued, 'I considered bringing chocolates, flowers or champagne, then I thought of a better gift that explains how I feel about things, how I feel about you.'

I sat there with my heart pounding, my mind whirring with a hundred thoughts, taking in what he was saying and watching him take something from the inside pocket of his jacket.

'I've been carrying this around with me for a while,' he said. 'The entire summer in fact. Every time I went to throw it away I couldn't do it. I didn't know why and yet...I suppose I do. This was my last piece of hope that one day I'd make things right. And so I couldn't throw it away because if I did I'd be throwing you away, and I couldn't do that.'

He presented me with a paint chart. A folded leaflet that looked like it had been in his pocket for months. It was a chart for pastel-coloured paints suitable for painting a shed.

'I picked it up after we'd chatted about your shed envy and I'd offered you my shed.' He pointed to the chart. 'It's non–smelly. The paint, not the chart which probably has a whiff of aftershave.'

I opened it and gazed at the colours. He'd chosen well. This was exactly the type of colours I'd had in mind for the shed.

He leaned down, almost nervously, as I still hadn't given him my reaction to everything he'd said. 'The pale blue is nice.' He pointed to it.

I nodded. 'It is, isn't it?'

Inside, all the feelings I had for Marck, the things I'd hoped for, even though I barely admitted it to myself, rose to the surface. I almost burst into tears but stopped myself.

'So what do you think?' he said gently.

I took a steadying breath. 'I think this is better than chocolates, flowers and champagne,' I managed to say.

'I'll buy you those too,' he added.

'There's no need.' I gazed up at him and smiled. 'I've got everything I need right here.'

He pulled me close and kissed me, and it felt like the first time, our time in Cornwall.

'Since the first day I saw you at the sewing bee, I haven't been able to get you out of my thoughts, Morag. I feel differently.'

'About what?'

'About everything,' he said. 'I can't settle back into my old life. I don't fit there any longer. I've tried. But I keep thinking about you, us, in Cornwall. That day in the sea with you is part of me forever. But seeing you having a sewing day with my mother and Zinnia was what changed everything really. You looked happy and content. So did they. And that made me feel content. And I don't feel like that. I'm always chasing the next shirt collection, flirting, causing trouble, making false promises. I used to be okay with that. Now I'd rather feel contentment, and that comes from being with you, Morag.'

'Letting Ruary affect my decisions was my mistake,' I told him. 'I can't believe that I even hesitated in replying to the email. You didn't push me into accepting the new contract, you just reminded me of what I'd have done before. I'd have accepted it immediately. I didn't need Ruary's permission.'

'Let's put it all in the past,' he said. His arms wrapped around my waist and he gave me a squeeze.

I stood on my tiptoes and kissed him. 'Let's do that.'

Zinnia was delighted for us, as were the ladies at the sewing bee when they found out we were a couple. Jannet and Denice were making a success of their sewing classes, along with Sharla who helped them part–time. They were still dating the lighting engineers from the fashion show, and Sharla had a new boyfriend.

As for Marck and me, we'd become inseparable. In more ways than one...

I cycled through the centre of Glasgow at 6:00 p.m. on a Monday night. The October air was crisp and it was one of those autumn evenings that has a sense of excitement to it.

'Where did you say the paint shop is?' I called to Marck.

'Second road on the left. They're open late on Mondays.'

We pedalled the tandem bicycle fast to get ahead of the traffic. The vintage bicycle for two was his idea. I liked being in front steering where we went.

'I've changed my mind about the eau–de–nil,' he called to me. 'I think the pale blue or vanilla would be lovely for your shed. I've even taken a liking to the lilac.'

I wasn't sure about the lilac. 'What's wrong with the eau–de–nil?'

'It's a bit greenish.'

'Eau–de–nil is green, Marck.'

'I know that.'

'You said I could paint the shed any colour I wanted. You said I should consider it my shed.'

'I did. Paint it green if you prefer.'

'I prefer the blue, though the lilac could be lovely.'

'It is.'

I breathed in the autumn air. I realised I'd have to wear my woolly hat soon when we were out on our bike. But that night I was happy to feel the breeze whip through my hair and anticipate buying pots of pastel–coloured paint. 'I'm looking forward to decorating my shed.'

'You do realise something,' he said.

'What?' I hoped he wasn't going to suggest decorating the shed with wallpaper.

'I'm going to have to make an honest woman of you.'

'I've been almost totally honest with you about nearly everything, Marck.'

'Honest as is...marriage.'

'Marriage?'

'Yes, you know that thing people do when they love each other and want to be together forever.'

'Oh that thing?'

'Yes, it's traditional.'

'We're very traditional,' I agreed with him, and steered the bicycle up the second street on the left. Or was it the third?

'We are. So at first I thought we could have one of those large weddings that take years to plan, then I thought we could run off to a tropical location and get wed there, then I thought no, we should get married in Scotland. We could get married at the cottage or my house or your shed. You may want to take that into consideration when painting it so that it matches the napkins and wedding invitations.'

I nodded. 'I'm now thinking the lilac.'

'Or the pale blue.'

We laughed and then I swerved to avoid a rut in the road.

'Turn around,' he called to me. 'This is a one–way street.'

'Is it?' I looked around for the sign which was probably a quarter of a street behind us at the rate we were going.

'Yes.'

I slowed down and turned the bike around. I glanced back and smiled at Marck. 'Whatever would I do without you?'

He smiled at me. 'I have no intention of letting you ever find out.'

End

About the Author:

Follow De-ann on Instagram @deann.black

De-ann Black is a bestselling author, scriptwriter and former newspaper journalist. She has over 80 books published. Romance, crime thrillers, espionage novels, action adventure. And children's books (non-fiction rocket science books and children's fiction). She became an Amazon All-Star author in 2014 and 2015.

She previously worked as a full-time newspaper journalist for several years. She had her own weekly columns in the press. This included being a motoring correspondent where she got to test drive cars every week for the press for three years.

Before being asked to work for the press, De-ann worked in magazine editorial writing everything from fashion features to social news. She was the marketing editor of a glossy magazine. She is also a professional artist and illustrator. Fabric design, dressmaking, sewing, knitting and fashion are part of her work.

Additionally, De-ann has always been interested in fitness, and was a fitness and bodybuilding champion, 100 metre runner and mountaineer. As a former N.A.B.B.A. Miss Scotland, she had a weekly fitness show on the radio that ran for over three years.

De-ann trained in Shukokai karate, boxing, kickboxing, Dayan Qigong and Jiu Jitsu. She is currently based in Scotland.
Her colouring books and embroidery design books are available in paperback. These include Floral Nature Embroidery Designs and Scottish Garden Embroidery Designs.

Also by De-ann Black (Romance, Action/Thrillers & Children's books). See her Amazon Author page or website for further details about her books, screenplays, illustrations, art and fabric designs.
www.De-annBlack.com

Romance books:

Sewing, Crafts & Quilting series:
1. The Sewing Bee
2. The Sewing Shop

Quilting Bee & Tea Shop series:
1. The Quilting Bee
2. The Tea Shop by the Sea

Heather Park: Regency Romance

Snow Bells Haven series:
1. Snow Bells Christmas
2. Snow Bells Wedding

Summer Sewing Bee
Christmas Cake Chateau

Cottages, Cakes & Crafts series:
1. The Flower Hunter's Cottage
2. The Sewing Bee by the Sea
3. The Beemaster's Cottage
4. The Chocolatier's Cottage
5. The Bookshop by the Seaside

Sewing, Knitting & Baking series:
1. The Tea Shop
2. The Sewing Bee & Afternoon Tea
3. The Christmas Knitting Bee
4. Champagne Chic Lemonade Money
5. The Vintage Sewing & Knitting Bee

The Tea Shop & Tearoom series:
1. The Christmas Tea Shop & Bakery
2. The Christmas Chocolatier
3. The Chocolate Cake Shop in New York at Christmas
4. The Bakery by the Seaside
5. Shed in the City

Tea Dress Shop series:
1. The Tea Dress Shop At Christmas
2. The Fairytale Tea Dress Shop In Edinburgh
3. The Vintage Tea Dress Shop In Summer

Christmas Romance series:
1. Christmas Romance in Paris.
2. Christmas Romance in Scotland.

Romance, Humour, Mischief series:
1. Oops! I'm the Paparazzi
2. Oops! I'm A Hollywood Agent
3. Oops! I'm A Secret Agent
4. Oops! I'm Up To Mischief

The Bitch-Proof Suit series:
1. The Bitch-Proof Suit
2. The Bitch-Proof Romance
3. The Bitch-Proof Bride

The Cure For Love
Dublin Girl
Why Are All The Good Guys Total Monsters?
I'm Holding Out For A Vampire Boyfriend

Action/Thriller books:
Love Him Forever
Someone Worse
Electric Shadows
The Strife Of Riley
Shadows Of Murder
Cast a Dark Shadow

Children's books:
Faeriefied
Secondhand Spooks
Poison-Wynd
Wormhole Wynd
Science Fashion
School For Aliens

Colouring books:
Flower Nature
Summer Garden
Spring Garden
Autumn Garden
Sea Dream
Festive Christmas
Christmas Garden
Christmas Theme
Flower Bee
Wild Garden
Faerie Garden Spring
Flower Hunter
Stargazer Space
Bee Garden
Scottish Garden Seasons

Embroidery Design books:
Floral Nature Embroidery Designs
Scottish Garden Embroidery Designs

Printed in Great Britain
by Amazon